The Weakness

Even the book morphs!
Flip the pages
and check it out!

titles in Large-Print Editions:

The Weakness

K.A. Applegate

Gareth Stevens Publishing
A WORLD ALMANAC EDUCATION GROUP COMPANY

Please visit our web site at: www.garethstevens.com
For a free color catalog describing Gareth Stevens' list
of high-quality books and multimedia programs, call
1-800-542-2595 (USA) or 1-800-461-9120 (Canada).
Gareth Stevens Publishing's Fax: (414) 332-3567.

Library of Congress Cataloging-in-Publication Data

Applegate, K. A.
　　The weakness / by K. A. Applegate.—North American ed.
　　　　p. cm. — (Animorphs)
　　Summary: When Tobias discovers Visser Three's newest
feeding place, the Animorphs must decide how to proceed.
　　ISBN 0-8368-2770-8 (lib. bdg.)
　　[1. Extraterrestrial beings—Fiction.　2. Science fiction.]
I. Title.
PZ7.A6483We　　2001
[Fic]—dc21　　　　　　　　　　　　　　　00-063543

This edition first published in 2001 by
Gareth Stevens Publishing
A World Almanac Education Group Company
330 West Olive Street, Suite 100
Milwaukee, WI　53212　USA

Published by Gareth Stevens, Inc., 330 West Olive Street,
Suite 100, Milwaukee, Wisconsin 53212 in large print by
arrangement with Scholastic Inc., 555 Broadway, New York,
New York 10012.

© 2000 by Katherine Applegate.

Cover illustration by David B. Mattingly.
Art Direction/Design by Karen Hudson.

ANIMORPHS is a registered trademark of Scholastic Inc.

Printed in the United States of America

1 2 3 4 5 6 7 8 9 05 04 03 02 01

The author wishes to thank Elise Smith for her help in preparing this manuscript.

For Michael and Jake

CHAPTER 1

My name is Rachel.

There's a person in the Bible named Rachel.

I don't know if my being called Rachel has anything to do with her. I doubt it. I've never seen my parents reading the Bible.

There's a Rachel on *Friends.* What's up with this season's stringy hair? Weird.

And there are, at any given time, approximately five Rachels in my school. At least two of whom are failing phys ed.

Maybe your name is Rachel, too.

It's a popular name. Lots of girls have it. Even girls who can manage to throw a basketball through a hoop from the foul line.

1

But I'm different from every other Rachel you've ever met.

And it's not just because the dorkier kids in school think I have a seriously bad attitude. Which I do. So what?

My being different from every other kid named Rachel is not necessarily a good thing. Or a bad thing. It just . . . is.

Sometimes — very rarely — I wish I were just one of the thousands of Rachels out there living an average life. One of the mass of average kids in average middle schools in average, all-American towns.

Actually, I wish that very, very rarely. I'm not thrilled with average. I don't do average well.

It's only when I'm seriously exhausted that — for about half a second — I wish I were just an ordinary Rachel. Like when I've been going on no sleep for forty-eight hours. When I've been slashing and shredding the enemy and leaking blood from my own gaping wounds until I can hardly breathe without it hurting. When the very thought of sleep seems totally foreign.

Sleep? Huh?

I don't wish it after a typical, everyday kind of mission. Just after the really annoying ones. The ones where we lose more than we gain. The ones where we fail to do any serious damage to the Yeerks.

Then, I wish — for about half a second — I were nobody special.

That I'd never stumbled onto the tragic sight of a dying alien warrior prince.

That he'd never told us about the Yeerk invasion of Earth. That he'd never chosen us — me, my cousin Jake, my best friend Cassie, Jake's best bud Marco, and this shy, compelling kid named Tobias — to adopt the noble Andalite mission.

That he'd never given us the gift and curse of Andalite morphing technology. The ability to touch an animal and absorb its DNA, all for the purpose of becoming that animal when necessary.

To fight off the invaders. To stave off the fate that has befallen so many other worlds throughout the universe.

A fate worse than death.

Total subservience to a mind-controlling master race.

You know what really infuriates me? This powerful enemy doesn't even stand on its own two feet.

The Yeerks are a race of parasitic slugs. No ears, eyes, mouths. No arms or legs. Just gray, viscous flesh. And the repulsive ability — need, really — to attach their otherwise helpless bodies to the brains of sentient creatures. To slither into the head through the ear canal. To flatten, lengthen, press themselves into every crevice

3

and wrinkle of the brain. Like clay being pushed into a mold.

And once there, to possess the person like a demon. Read all memories. Know all secrets. Control all movements. Basically use that host body for its own evil purpose. To capture more and more host bodies for more and more Yeerk parasites.

Without us humans — and without the Gedds and Hork-Bajir and Taxxons — the Yeerks are nothing on this planet. Fat, wormlike creatures swimming dully in a Yeerk pool. Blind. Deaf. Circling endlessly.

Problem is, they have us. Some of us, anyway. Some humans. Most Hork-Bajir. All Taxxons. One Andalite.

<Rachel?>

Now was not one of those times when I wished I were just an average, ordinary Rachel. Now I was ticked. And being ticked is one of the stand-out things about being me.

I do anger well.

<Rachel, if I might express an opinion I suspect will deeply annoy you . . .>

"Spit it out, Ax."

Aximili Esgarrouth-Isthill. Younger brother of Prince Elfangor Sirinial-Shamtul, the guy who dragged us into this war. Andalite. Our friend, too.

<I would be happy to comply. However, I can-

not perform the action humans call "spitting" for the simple fact that at the moment I do not have mouthparts. . . .>

"What were you going to say, Ax?" Cassie, stepping in before I could do something stupid like pop him one. You don't want to get into an unnecessary fight with a guy who sports a big ole blade on the end of a very fast-moving tail.

And I've been known to get into fights some people would call unnecessary.

<Prince Jake left no specific instructions in his temporary absence. I am of the opinion he would prefer us not to act without his knowledge.>

Jake was away for a few days. Visiting some relative of his, not mine. Tom stayed at home so at least Jake didn't have to face that whole "do I kill my brother to save my father" thing again.

Tom is a Controller. Which means he has a Yeerk in his head.

I groaned. "Look, Ax. It's an opportunity. We need opportunities. We don't pick and choose them like they're — like they're blouses on a rack. We take the chance. Even if it's got a few loose threads. Or a hole."

What was the problem? Why couldn't they see . . .

<Rachel's right,> said Tobias, from his lookout perch in the rafters. We were in Cassie's

5

barn. <We know Visser Three changes feeding places regularly. We have two, three days tops before we lose him again. It was luck I found his current site. I say we do it. Try to take him down.>

"Gotta agree with Bird-boy on this, Ax-man," Marco said. "You feel you can't act without a direct order, you can sit this one out."

<I will be there,> Ax said quickly.

"Cassie?"

"Honestly, I'd rather wait for Jake. But I'm in. And I know the perfect morph for the job. The Gardens just got three cheetahs as part of their new breeding program. You know, they're almost extinct."

"Why cheetahs?" I asked.

"Speed. You want to grab the visser quickly, before his guards can react," Cassie explained. "You want to outrun him in an open space. And pretty much nothing outruns a cheetah."

I grinned. This was cool.

The bad missions, I hate. But I'm never happier than when starting out on an important mission — especially one that was going to be so easy.

CHAPTER 2

Tobias led us to the visser's new temporary feeding pasture. The five of us flew out, careful to keep the red-tailed hawk in sight and careful to stay enough apart not to arouse suspicion.

Me in bald eagle morph. Cassie and Marco as osprey. Ax as northern harrier. In nature, these birds don't make a habit of hanging together.

The pasture was really a small valley, tucked away in the foothills of the mountains. Charming. Lush green grass. Bright yellow wildflowers. Soft breezes.

The perfect place for the most evil being in this or any galaxy to claim as his own.

That was supposed to be funny or ironic or something.

As planned, we landed at various points on the perimeter of the valley. Four of us would morph to cheetah.

Tobias would stay hawk and act as lookout and guide, directing our assault.

<There it is,> Tobias said. <Right on schedule. At the far end of the valley. See how the air shimmers?>

Through the eagle's incredibly keen eyes I saw the visser's Blade ship. The cloaking device that had kept it hidden on its journey to the valley was lifting, revealing the grim, battle-ax-shaped vehicle, its two huge scimitarlike wings flared out behind the main body.

The ship fairly oozed a sense of dark and evil.

<I'm going on record that I so do not like this,> Marco said from across the valley.

<Tough. Everybody, demorph!> I demanded. <We are going to take him down.>

I concentrated and felt the changes begin.

ZWOOOP!

I shot up from the ground, a sudden, bizarrely tall eagle.

Brown wings with a combined extension of six feet became my shorter human arms.

Deadly talons became harmless five-toed feet.

The eagle's white feathered head grew and sprouted long blond hair. Eyes widened and vision blurred.

When I was done, I took a deep breath and thought: *cheetah*. Quite possibly the most gorgeous wild cat ever to roam the savannah.

Like time-release photography. The tawny, black-spotted fur of the cheetah shot out of my fingertips and crawled its way up my fingers, across my hands, up my arms.

Beautiful!

Thickening. Now down my legs. And across my broad feline chest, whiter fur with fewer spots.

I looked at Cassie, closest to me, and watched as black tear-tracks drew themselves from the inner corners of her golden cheetah eyes to the bottom of her top jaw.

Like a thick black Magic Marker being swept down a page.

Like a bandit's mask.

A tickling — and I could feel similar marks being drawn on my own feline face. Down from eyes that saw in a wide-angle view.

I dropped to my knees, ready.

BOOIIINNGGG!

My spine elongated. Became amazingly flexible. A spine that acted like a spring.

Coil. Stretch! Coil. Stretch! Allowing my back legs to push harder against the grass. My long, slender front legs to extend way out. To reach for my prey.

9

So that I could knock it down before strangling it.

POOOF!

My lungs, huge and powerful, inflated like a balloon.

Air!

Breathing had never been so . . . easy. So satisfying. I drew enormous amounts of air into my lungs. Effortless. My huge heart pumped oxygen to every muscle in my body.

POP! POP!

The dewclaw. One on each front paw, but off the ground. Sharp. Useful for smacking down fleet-of-foot gazelles and other four-legged prey.

POPPOPPOPPOPPOP!

Other claws — blunt, hard, and nonretractable — gripped the dirt. Nails like a dog's. Hard, sharp toe pads — natural cleats — pushed out from the bottom of my four paws.

Surefooted. This was traction Jeff Gordon would envy. I could turn, forty-five degrees, at full speed, fifty, sixty miles an hour, and not slide.

I was the professional athlete of felines.

One hundred and forty pounds of muscle and grace.

WHOOOSSSHHH!

My tail!

Long, half the length of my body, and muscular. Thick. Spots fading into stripes at the white tip. Unique markings, distinguishing me from every other cheetah.

My tail, an amazing stabilizer, helping my four-and-a-half-foot-long body maneuver during the crucial twenty-second chase.

Cut right. Cut left. Twist. Turn. All without slowing or falling.

I was built for speed. Not endurance, maybe. But oh, yes. Definitely speed.

Stunning speed.

Zero to forty-five miles per hour in two point five seconds.

From a point of rest. From sitting perfectly still.

Do you understand that kind of acceleration? I mean, can you even really imagine it?

And once the cheetah got going — top speed, between sixty and seventy miles per hour — it could cover almost one hundred feet per second.

Per second!

Okay, try this. Just put one foot in front of the other and walk off one hundred feet. It won't be exact but it'll be close enough.

While you're walking off those hundred steps, keep track of how long it takes you.

Probably about a minute, give or take.

Now, when you've walked off those hundred feet, turn and look back to where you started.

11

A cheetah would have covered that same distance in one second.

Almost like magic.

I'm here.

One second.

I'm there!

I survey my domain. I spot my prey.

I stalk.

I dash!

Like lightning!

I smack down my victim. I bite out its throat.

Visser Three didn't stand a chance.

This mission would count. This mission would matter. This time, *they* would bleed.

CHAPTER 3

<H>ere he comes,> Tobias warned. <Everybody in place. He's moving toward the door of the ship. Almost . . . almost there . . .>

Visser Three, in his stolen Andalite body, the only Yeerk ever to have forced an Andalite to be his host, stepped through the doorway of the ship. He surveyed the valley. Then he nodded to the four Hork-Bajir who flanked the ramp and descended.

<Wait until he's, like, ten, fifteen yards away from the ship,> I said. <Then we hit. One right after the other. First me. Then Ax. Then Marco. Then Cassie.>

<Okay, Xena,> Marco said. <You want to run this show, fine.>

13

<This morph wants to break out,> Cassie said. <I'm ready.>

The four of us surrounded the visser. Crouched low in the gently bending grasses and wildflowers of the valley.

The plan was to take him down. To attack with deadly speed and accuracy. Four lean, powerfully muscled Earth hunters against one alien prey. Ha! By the time the Hork-Bajir guards could take ten steps from the ship, Dracon beams leveled, the visser would be dead.

Closer. Head held high, Visser Three stepped off the ramp and onto the grass. Testing its flavor through his Andalite hooves. Finding it good.

Nodding and walking more boldly onto the field. Until . . .

<Now!> Tobias cried.

I sprang.

Up and out of the protective covering of the long grass. Zero to forty-five mph. Two point five seconds.

It was true. Every unbelievable fact I knew about this cat was true!

I shot toward the visser. His four eyes faced forward, but not for long. He saw me coming, on his left. At least, he saw something. A blur.

He stopped. Began to turn sharply right and —
WHACK!

I hit his rear left leg with my right front paw!

14

He stumbled. I ducked away from his bladed tail and reached out again.

WHACK!

He was down! On his knees!

Good. I was already tiring. Just slightly.

The visser stumbled to his feet! Okay, he was tougher than a gazelle. No problem because . . .

Ax!

Unreal! My wide-angle vision caught a golden blur on my left — and then another on the right. And another.

I raced again after the visser.

We circled him. Four powerful, swift cheetahs running dizzying circles around one scrambling Andalite, frantically kicking up clods of grass and soil, his tail blade thwacking only air.

We were going to do it!

We were going to take him down!

One of us — just one of us — had to slip in under that Andalite tail, smack him down, go for the throat . . .

<Hork-Bajir!> Tobias called.

TSEEEW! TSEEEW!

Dracon beams whizzed past us. We dodged them without really trying.

<We're too fast for their weapons!> I crowed.

<But once we slow or stop, we are vulnerable,> Ax said, slinking closer toward the visser, causing him to slide and stumble.

15

<And the cheetah's tiring,> Cassie said.

I felt it, too. The cat was almost ready to collapse. Its endurance was almost gone.

<Only the four Hork-Bajir,> Tobias called.

<Then we take our chances, now!> I commanded. <On the count of three we dive for the visser and . . .>

<AAAHHHH!>

One of us had been hit! Slashed by a bold Hork-Bajir guard who'd rushed us, too suddenly for Tobias to have anticipated. Blood poured from a nasty wound on the cheetah's back.

<I'm hit!> Marco.

SLASH! Another Hork-Bajir, dropping his Dracon beam, throwing himself into the fight. We would be fatally lacerated in moments! No way could blunt nails and a dewclaw do real damage to the tough, leathery skin of the Yeerk shock troops. Before our teeth could reach their throats we'd be sliced luncheon meat.

<Finally! You imbeciles!> the visser screamed.

No choice. I batted a Hork-Bajir. Missed. Tried to strike again. My lungs felt as if they were about to collapse.

SLASH! SLASH!

<RACHEL!> Tobias cried.

I slunk rapidly away from my attacker, blood streaming into my eyes. Saw Marco and Ax and Cassie valiantly defending our prey — the visser —

and failing. Panting, practically dragging them-selves along the torn-up ground to avoid another Hork-Bajir swipe.

We were losing!

No.

<Once more!> I shouted. <Grab . . .>

WHOOOOOOSSH!

I fell, face forward, tumbled hind legs over head. I was hit! Hit by . . . something. Knocked over hard by the blast of wind that followed in its wake.

Whatever it was.

CHAPTER 4

ШHOOOOOOOSSH!

I climbed to my feet.

Tried to leap after it.

Where was it? There!

Only air!

THUUMPF!

I fell again.

WHOOOOOOOSSSH!

<I can't even see it!> Cassie cried.

ZZIIIIISSSSSPPP!

<See what?> asked Marco. <A-uumpfh!>

In seconds — if that — it had us herded into a trembling, panting, tangled cluster. Four incredibly fast, incredibly agile hunters, subdued.

18

The thing made me think of pulled taffy.

Or of a cartoon depiction of speed.

You know, where the cartoon character's skin stretches as he strides faster and faster — until his skeleton runs right out of its skin suit.

That's where this thing belonged. In a cartoon. Where the impossible is possible.

An impression. A flash. A blur.

A small whirlwind or tornado.

And then it stopped. Suddenly.

Came to a dead clean halt. No slowing down. Just — stopped.

<What the . . .>

It was a creature. Now I could see that clearly. Not a machine but flesh and blood.

A bizarre creature able to zip across the grass like a high-speed insect.

Like a bullet fired from a thirty-thirty. A hunting rifle.

Only about as tall as a gazelle.

Four lanky, skinny legs. A thin but strong-looking tail, as long as its body, that flicked and twitched even when the creature's legs weren't moving.

A pigeon chest, high and rounded.

A head shaped like a custom-made aerodynamic bike racing helmet. Tight curved face, like half a smooth ball. Skull that swept back from the rim of this ball into a pointy triangle. Like an ice cream cone on its side. Except the cone was flattened.

But what really caught and held my attention was the fact that this thing was covered in blue fur.

And had no mouth.

And sported two thin, weak-looking arms.

Like an Andalite. Like Ax.

<Bail! Just go!> Tobias called frantically. <I'll distract it.>

But Tobias didn't have to distract it. The creature suddenly left us — and appeared at the bedraggled visser's side. In the time it took to blink.

<Now!> I cried.

We ran, fear and the dregs of adrenaline helping the exhausted cheetahs to relative safety, scattered throughout the thick woods surrounding the valley.

We got away only because the creature had let us. I knew that.

And I didn't like it one bit. It made me angry. More annoying, it made me nervous.

Why had it let us get away?

We demorphed, on our way to our usual bird morphs for the trip home.

And we listened to the creature speak with Visser Three.

Thought-speak. Superfast.

The words became clear a beat after the creature had stopped speaking. A time delay between
sound and meaning.

Kind of like when you talk on the phone to
someone in Europe. Or any other continent, I
guess.

<Apatheticdisplay,VisserThree.Youarechased
downonaplanetyoushouldlongagohaveconquer-
ed.Thiswillgoinmynotesyoucanbesure.>

<You, too, failed to capture the Andalite ban-
dits, Inspector,> the visser sneered. Loudly.

<Depriveyouofwhatisyourdutyandresponsibil-
ity? Andmyenjoymentinwatchingyoufail?Finally,
youwilladdressmeasCouncilorThirteen,Visser.>

<You're not a member of the council, yet. Not
until you have received final approval,> the visser
stated flatly.

The inspector made a sound that could have
been a laugh. High and trilling. A sound that sent
chills up my temporarily human spine.

<Ihavebeengivenaspecimenofournewestand
mostcapablehostspecies.TheGaratron.Iwillnotfail
tobepromoted.>

Kneeling on the dark soil, my back bent, hair
hanging down over my face, a twig imbedding itself into the skin of my right palm. A human
palm.

Still feeling, strangely, some of the cheetah's
exhaustion.

21

But it was too dangerous to delay. I took a deep breath and rushed right into the next morph.

In what seemed like seconds, I had brown-and-white feathers, massive wings, a hard, cruel beak.

I was a bald eagle.

<Everyone?> I called privately. <Take off, one at a time. I'll go last. Tobias first, Ax, Marco, and Cassie. Meet back at the barn.>

<Rachel?> It was Tobias. <I'll wait for you.>

CHAPTER 5

<Councilor,> Ax said, his voice tight. <The inspector is a candidate member of the Council of Thirteen.>

"What's this guy doing here?" I said angrily. "He screwed up our plan."

Marco turned to look at Ax. "Did you know about these Garatrons?" he asked. "I mean, I know I'm not the only one who saw the similarities. Blue fur. Four legs. Arms."

Ax stiffened.

"Physical similarities don't necessarily mean there's a genetic relationship," Cassie pointed out. "Mammalian shrews and marsupial shrews. A lot alike, but not related. Could be the same thing with Andalites and Garatrons."

<The Yeerks have taken only one Andalite host body,> Ax said. <The inspector called the Garatrons the newest host species, implying the Yeerks have infested far more than one creature. Something the Andalites will never allow to happen.>

I paced before a cage full of chittering baby squirrels. Their mother had been killed.

"This is bad. The inspector outran one of the fastest, most agile animals on Earth. If we can't catch the Garatrons, we can't kill them."

<We're missing something here,> Tobias said. <I don't know about other Garatrons, but the inspector, the Yeerk, is very intelligent. That much was obvious. And he and the visser were antagonistic. That was clear, too. The inspector mentioned notes. I'm betting he's here to observe Visser Three. Make and submit a progress report on the invasion of Earth.>

I thought about what Tobias had said. It made sense. But what did it mean for us? And how could we exploit the visser's being under a microscope? Later on we could deal with the implications of yet another gifted Yeerk host species. Maybe when Jake came back.

And then I grinned. "This is so perfect. This is another opportunity."

Cassie looked up from the droppers of milk or

something she was preparing for the squirrel babies. "To do . . . ?"

"To discredit Visser Three. Embarrass him in front of the inspector. Show the inspector what an incredibly lousy job the visser's doing. Get him kicked off the job."

Marco raised his hand. "Wait up. And what happens when Visser Three is gone? Assuming, of course, we succeed. What if the council replaces him with someone far more dangerous?"

<Better the evil you know than the evil you don't know,> Tobias said quietly.

Cassie nodded. "Maybe. But I want to hear what Rachel has in mind."

"Simple," I said. "A kind of smear campaign. We strike hard and fast. Continuous pressure. Make it look like there's five hundred Andalite bandits fighting this war. We hit every known Controller in town. Every one in a position of power, anyway. And we hit in public places, wherever there's a Controller in charge. We want coverage. We want the inspector to know what's going on. And we do it now. We don't know how long the inspector is going to be here. We start today!"

"I say we wait," Marco said abruptly. "When's Jake getting back? Two, three days? We wait. I like the idea, Rachel, but this mission is potentially too dangerous to do without him."

"What's so dangerous?" I argued. "Boom boom boom. We hit, we get out. We hit again."

"Yeah, in totally open, public places." Marco shook his head. "You amaze me. How can you not see the risk in that? The chance that one of us will get left behind? That one of us will have to demorph in the middle of a supermarket bread aisle with a Yeerk-infested stock boy peeking around the hamburger roll display, waiting to drag us off to Visser Three?"

<Or not be able to demorph,> Tobias said, his voice forcedly arch and bright. <Or maybe be captured and tortured.>

I shot him a look. It pained me when he talked like that. He didn't do it often, but . . .

Tobias had been caught in morph, way back in the beginning. More recently, he'd been voluntarily captured, for the sake of the mission. Tortured, too. He'd sacrificed more than any of us for this stupid war. He had a right to deal with it all whatever way he could.

Still, it hurt me to see him reveal the damage that had been done to him. I have strong feelings for Tobias. The kind you can't help. The kind that seem inevitable. Like they were always there, even before you knew the person.

"I agree with Marco and Tobias," Cassie said, opening the door of the squirrels' cage. "It's a good idea. But for a fast series of relentless attacks we need someone calling the shots. And Jake does that better than anyone."

"Jake's not here," I grumbled.

"And look what's happening," Cassie went on, over her shoulder. "We're wasting time arguing. Without a leader, nothing gets done."

"My point exactly," I said. "So let's choose a temporary leader. Look, we're agreed we can't go into a mission arguing over who's in charge and when. So . . ."

<But are we agreed we should go ahead? If someone acts as leader?> Tobias said. <Ax?>

<I must decline to contribute my opinion. And I must decline to participate in the choosing of a leader to substitute for my prince. This is a matter for you humans to decide.>

<I'm not denying the danger,> Tobias said slowly. <But like Rachel said, we've got a solid opportunity. The risks are big. But I'm not sure we're free to say no.>

"And Rachel's also saying she wants to be in charge, right?" Marco. "I mean, that's what this is really all about, right?"

I bit back an angry response. If I wanted to lead, I had to control myself first. "No. That's not what I'm saying." I turned to Cassie. "I don't care who's in charge. Cassie can be in charge."

Cassie fitted a dropper into a little squirrel mouth. "No thanks. Brain surgery? Okay. Secret rescue missions to the Yeerk pool? When I have to. But not this kind of thing. Not rapid-fire attacks."

"Tobias?" I said. "How about you?"

<No. I'm no one's leader.>

"Much as I hate to admit anyone is superior to me," Marco sighed, "I'd have to say that in terms of intelligence, Ax is our man."

Ax tilted his head back almost as if he were posing for a photo shoot.

"But," Marco went on, "and no offense, Ax-man, this job is going to require pretty intimate contact with humans. With, uh, society. And let's face it, you still don't accept Earth hours as your own hours. And your favorite TV shows are 'These Messages.' Not good."

Ax looked offended. <I will abide by whatever decision the — >

"So who's left?" I challenged. "You?"

"Possibly."

"Not likely. I'm the one who does hard and fast. And relentless."

"And reckless," Marco shot back.

"While you want to sit around and think every stupid little step to death," I spat. "You've got a Hamlet complex, Marco."

"Yeah and there's a method to my madness. Which is more than I can say about your finer moments."

<Who or what is this Hamlet complex?> Ax asked.

"I'll explain later," Cassie said quickly. "Look, if we're going to have a leader until Jake gets back, we're going to have to choose that leader in the democratic way. We are a team, right?"

<A vote,> Tobias said. <It's the only way.>

Marco snorted. "Beautiful. Let's see. We've got Rachel's best friend and her bird-friend and Ax isn't voting . . . forget it, man. I'm out."

Marco turned to me and bowed. "Congratulations, your highness. Your wish is my command."

CHAPTER 6

"Crap."

I threw myself onto my back and folded my arms across my chest.

Sleep was just not going to happen. My mind was too busy whirling, racing. Thinking about the strangest things.

Not about the first attack we'd planned, on the local Yeerk-controlled TV station.

But about how last month in English class we studied a few Greek tragedies. Like *Oedipus Rex.* Written by a guy with an equally unpronounceable name.

That's where I first heard the word "hubris."

Hubris is like a disease. It means excessive pride. Over-the-top self-confidence. The belief that you can do anything you want, better than anyone else. Because you know best. Because you're special.

Because you're you.

The problem is, hubris usually results in some extremely nasty payback. Like being so horrified when you learn that something you did was really, really wrong that you pluck out your own eyes. It kind of scared me, reading about those heroes and warriors and kings.

It also kind of reassured me. Made me feel like I was part of a special club, one that's been around for a long time. An exclusive club. A club for people like me who know they can do great things and do them. And then get punished for doing them.

"Ugh."

I sat up and shoved the pillows behind my back. If I couldn't sleep I wasn't going to just lie there staring at the ceiling.

Maybe I would read. Or listen to the radio.

Why was I thinking about this stuff now anyway?

Because suddenly, I was the leader of our little band of soldiers. That's why.

And Jake had told me often enough that the leader can be as scared or full of doubt as any of his followers. He just isn't allowed to show it.

Under any circumstances.

31

No matter how horrible things get.

That's the deal. People want their leaders to be larger than life. Perfect. Not subject to human frailty and weaknesses. Gods.

"People want their leaders to act the way they wish they could act themselves," Jake always said. Totally confident. Completely brave. Not afraid. Never confused. Never worried.

Trouble was, I was confused. And majorly worried.

Being the leader is mostly about other people.

Being the kind of hero I was born to be — the kind of hero I'd discovered myself to be since this war started — was a lot about me.

I was smart enough to have figured that out. So I was worried. Suddenly and out of the blue. Worried I'd do something on this mission that would seriously backfire on one of my friends. Worried I'd be responsible for doing something so wrong I'd want to pluck out my own eyes, like that poor old Greek from the story.

It bothered me. Made me mad. I couldn't afford to worry. And I definitely couldn't afford to show it. I was the hero, the warrior, the king! The doer of great deeds! Right?

And in order to do the great things, in order to win wars and build cities, or whatever, you've got to have pride and confidence. You've got to be just a little bit arrogant. Sometimes a lot arrogant. Pride and confidence and arrogance equal courage. At least it was that way for me.

If we — we heroes and warriors and kings — didn't do the grisly but necessary stuff, the insanely brave stuff, who would?

"Nobody, that's who," I said to the sliver of moon peeping through the open curtains.

So it's a trap. An inevitability. You are who you are. Character is plot. Character is destiny.

TAP TAP TAP.

I swung out of bed and went to the window.

"Hey," I said, raising it to let Tobias walk in to perch on my desk. "What took you so long?"

<Sorry. Ax waylaid me. There was a dessert special on his favorite cooking show . . .>

"Tobias?" I interrupted. "Do you think we're doing the right thing? Rapid strikes I mean? Make the inspector think we're all over the visser's butt? That we're stronger than we really are? It's a good strategy, right?"

Tobias fixed me with his intense hawk stare. <Stealth wouldn't get us anywhere right now. We don't know exactly how long the inspector will be here. So if we're going to act, this seems the way to do it.>

"So, you think I'm right," I pressed. "That I'm the one for the job. I'm the one, right?"

Nothing.

It mattered very, very much what Tobias

33

thought. I knew he was my friend. I knew he loved me. I knew that much.

But tonight, more than usual, it mattered that he believed in me.

"I mean, you were going to vote for me, right?" I said quickly. "And Cassie . . ."

<I think we'd better get moving if we're going to meet the others before the morning news.>

For a minute I didn't say anything. Then I yanked my favorite old ratty nightgown off over my head and stood in the center of the moonlit room, shivering in my morphing suit.

"Fine. Let's do it."

CHAPTER 7

"You know, before I started hanging with you people, I didn't even know there was such a thing as sunrise. No, I mean it. I knew the sun set. And when I woke up each morning it was back in the sky. But the actual rising part . . ."

"Marco."

"I'm shutting up," he said, yawning and crouching.

We were in the alley behind the WKVT TV studio. First stop on our planned rampage. On our mission to convince the inspector that the Andalite bandits were all over the visser's butt, like white on rice.

Another mission that had us meddling in Yeerk politics.

I fought off a dark flash of doubt. Shot a look at Tobias. Did he not trust me? Shouldn't matter. Maybe that's what he was telling me: It shouldn't matter what he thought.

"Battle morphs," I said.

Marco stood. "Hold up, General Patton. How about step one, first?"

I scowled. "Am I the leader here?"

<Let's hear what Marco has to say,> Tobias said neutrally.

"Infiltration. None of us has ever been inside this place, right? We check it out in some small morph, get the layout, then if it looks safe, we do battle morphs."

I shook my head. "No. Not a good idea. That means we'd have to go human inside. Too risky."

"Unless we did flies. Something small, at least. Went in, scoped out the place, bailed, de-morphed, remorphed to battle morphs, and went back in," Cassie said.

"Why don't we just put off the mission until, say, next week?" I said nastily.

Cassie looked ticked off but I didn't care. "Ax, you're with me on this, right?"

<I agree with the "hammer" concept. That we work rapidly through our list of suggested targets. However . . .>

"Okay, battle morphs. We go in hard and fast.

Create havoc. Wreck the place. But try not to hurt anyone, okay?"

Marco sighed and began his morph to gorilla. "Uh-huh."

I began to morph to grizzly bear. And as I grew, larger, stronger, more dangerous, the doubts seemed to shrivel away. Marco was always dubious. Big deal. Forget Marco. And Tobias was . . . forget him, too. I was right.

Six feet tall, seven, more. Muscles on muscles. Bones so thick they could have been dinosaur fossils. Matted fur that was like a suit of armor. I was power made flesh. The most powerful land predator on planet Earth.

I was a grizzly bear.

<Okay, boys and girls. Let's kick it.>

I slammed into the door.

WHAM!

The door came off its hinges. It fell with a clatter.

We were in! A narrow hallway. Bright lights. Moving shapes and figures, all blurry to my weak eyes.

But we were in. Grizzly, gorilla, Andalite, wolf, and hawk — bent on destruction.

<Move! Move! Move!>

Down the hallway we tore.

A scream! Papers flung in panic. I swatted

down a framed picture and left gashes in the Sheetrock.

"What the . . . ?"

"Oh my God!"

I dropped to all fours and ran full-out. A bear on the move is like a semi on the interstate: Get out of the way.

I brushed a Xerox machine and sent it tumbling. Marco punched a side door and crumpled it in. A security guard loomed up, trying to draw his weapon.

FWAPP! Ax's tail cracked, fast as a bullwhip, and the guard fell unconscious to the floor.

A man with a clipboard. I hit him like a bowling ball hitting a pin. He rolled over my back and hit the floor. Cassie leaped nimbly over him.

Suddenly we were out of the hallway. Out in the open. Backstage. I could see the bracing for the set.

I reared up and shouldered into a big TV camera on a dolly. It went spinning and crashed into the back of the set.

<On to the set!> I was pumped. Exuberant. Nothing could stop us!

"Tseeer!"

"What the . . . Get those An — animals out of here!"

Ah. Christine Kaminsky. Our favorite Yeerkish morning news personality.

All dressed up in her tight but tasteful two-piece red suit and understated, expensive gold costume jewelry.

We'd caught her in the middle of her read-through. She looked really, really unhappy.

<Rip this place apart!> I cried.

<Easy on the people,> Cassie said. <Most are probably innocent.>

I jumped in one easy bound onto the anchor desk. It collapsed. I rolled away.

<Am I seeing snap-on hair on Bobby Baransky?!> Marco cried.

<Oh, I think so!> Cassie said, growling and backing Christine's blandly handsome weenie sidekick up onto his news desk.

CRASH!

Another news desk upended. I slid it across the floor and into the weather map "green screen" for good measure.

ZZEWEEEEEE . . . SSZZZZ . . .

Marco yanked microphones and other electronic equipment from the overhead grid while Ax went off to find the control room, pull some key levers and switches, and put WKVT off the air.

<We have company, guys,> Tobias called as he landed on an overhead lighting fixture.

I whirled as quickly as my shaggy brown mass would allow. Coming into the studio, led by an

39

employee guide, was a group of about twenty visitors. Adults and kids. I guess even local "personalities" have their fans.

The guide stopped cold. She screamed. She fainted. Grizzly sight isn't great, but I could make out most of the visitors standing frozen, mouths hanging open.

I turned back to the destruction. To the crew, long since scattered. To Christine and Bobby, now both huddled and crying behind Bobby's crumpled desk, menaced by Cassie's growling, snarling wolf.

I thwacked a rolling coffee cart with my big bear paw. Sent it careening into a wall. Bagels and pastries flew. A chocolate frosted donut rolled toward the visitors.

<Time to bail, Rachel,> Tobias said. <Too many civilians, now, with these tourists. Someone's going to get hurt.>

<No! Not yet!>

The seats for the occasional live audience were bolted to the floor, ten rows of five chairs each, one after the other up a slight incline.

RIIPP!

One less seat!

CRAASH!

The seat flew into the wall, knocking down a chunk of plaster the size of a truck tire.

Then, "Oh, no!" A vague voice from the cluster of onlookers. "Someone, help!" And, "Grandpa!"

<Rachel?> It was Ax. From the control room, unseen by the visitors. <I have accomplished my task. But I am hemmed in. There is a human with a gun. I do not wish to injure him.>

<Okay, Tobias, Cassie, cover Ax and then haul out of here,> I ordered. <Marco? Grab Miss Sunshine, there.>

Marco grabbed the screaming, resisting Yeerk anchorwoman by her blouse and held her motionless. I put my huge bear face up close to hers.

I give her credit: She had some courage.

"You don't scare me, Andalite," she hissed.

<Oh, but I do,> I said. <I have a message for Visser Three. Are you ready to hear it?>

She said nothing, just drew back from my teeth.

<Here's the message for the visser, and all your brother Yeerks: Go home. Can you remember that? Tell him we said, "Go home.">

I nodded to Marco. He released her. She straightened her clothes and glared hatred at us.

We were in the studio for less than five minutes. By the time we left, there was no studio.

We bailed, ran, and demorphed well away from the police cars, ambulances, and news vans that were racing toward the site.

41

<I believe this first raid met its goal,> Ax commented.

"I can't believe we had a live audience," Cassie said, laughing. "It was more than we could have hoped for. In one way." Suddenly, she didn't seem so sure. "Maybe it would have been better if we'd known they were in the building. Gotten them out first somehow."

There was a moment of weird silence. Like everyone was suddenly thinking real hard about those visitors.

<I saw one guy . . .> Tobias began, silent until now. <He fell. He was kind of old. What if he had a heart attack or whatever?>

I felt a chill. Something like fear. Or guilt. And then the chill was chased away by a hot rush of — something else. Self-defense? Something.

"Yeah, what if he just tripped? Come on. Casualties happen," I said coldly. "We didn't mean for the guy to get so scared. Besides, for all we know he's a Controller, too."

My team looked at me. And that weird silence was still hanging around.

But they had a job to do. And they'd just have to toughen up and do it.

"The raid was a success," I said. "End of story. Now, we have a schedule. Next stop, bookstore."

CHAPTER 8

We demorphed from birds behind the massive stacks of cardboard boxes in the alley behind the local bookstore.

"Somebody grab me a Laa-Laa doll when we're inside, okay?" Marco said. "I really like that little yellow one."

I gave him a look. You know the one.

"What?" he said defensively. "I'll send the manager a check tomorrow. Even though he's a Yeerk. It's not like I'm going to steal it or anything."

"Uh, Marco, you do know Teletubbies are for preschoolers, right?" Cassie said.

<"Eh-oh, Laa-Laa,"> Ax said. <"Big hug.">

<Okay, that does it, Ax,> Tobias grumbled. <We need to think about turning off your TV.>

<Remember,> Tobias said, <careful of the civilians. This time of day, should be mostly empty. But —>

I deliberately interrupted him. "We're in and out in five minutes tops," I reminded everyone. "Just like the studio. Five minutes of rock and roll. Ax? You keep us honest, okay?"

<Of course. But I was not aware that we would be involved in perpetrating a deception.>

<Just keep track of time for us, Ax,> Tobias said. <At four minutes, we get ready to bail.>

"Hey! I thought I was giving the orders," I blurted, annoyed.

Tobias turned slightly away and stared into space.

"I mean, am I wrong about that?"

"No, you're right. But you might want to consider one of those leadership workshops, Rachel," Marco said mildly. "The ones that teach communication skills. Like how not to be a jerk."

"We're ready when you give the word, Rachel," Cassie said calmly.

I let it go. No point getting into it with Marco. Or Tobias, for that matter. I was proving all I needed to prove.

"Let's do this," I said.

We morphed.

We tore in through the loading dock at the rear of the building. Grizzly, gorilla, wolf, hawk, and Andalite clopped and knuckle-walked and trotted through the stockrooms and employee locker rooms, tossing aside cardboard boxes, sending empty pallets careening into full shelves, and upending flimsy metal lockers.

Then we erupted out onto the main floor of the store and unleashed our own patented brand of havoc.

"Aaahhh!"

"Holy . . ."

"Help!"

I stabbed my X-Men Wolverine nails into a cardboard box of books and flung it. It ripped open in midair. Books flew, and I wanted to laugh.

The three employees at the cash registers decided it was time to leave. They left. Very quickly. One left his cash drawer open. I ran behind the counter and slammed the drawer shut. This was not about looting. No one was going to steal money and blame us.

No stealing. Plenty of mayhem.

"Tseeer!" Tobias!

Ha!

Hunched over, his hands on his head, the

ultrahip twenty-something manager Tobias had identified as a Yeerk the week before scuttled into a corner like a panicked bug!

A crowd of patrons stampeded for the front door of the store. One guy threw himself against a wall shelf and climbed it like a ladder. Cassie chased the shoppers to the door, then turned to snap and growl at the retreating heels of the climber. She was trying to keep them out of the way. Trying to make sure none of them played the hero and got hurt.

"My chai! Nooooo . . ."

From the little café where Ax was cutting seat cushions into threads, cups of espresso and double mocha latte and hot chocolate were being tossed into the air. Brown foamy liquid rained down like sizzling polluted rain.

It was panic! It was chaos! It was hysterical!

And I was responsible!

THUDDD!

Marco, in the children's department.

He sent wire and cardboard racks crashing to the floor. Two-foot-high brightly colored displays snapped off as the racks hit the ground. *Guess How Much I Love You* bunnies slamming down on top of assorted Disney heroines and Pooh and Piglet and Tigger . . .

CRASH!

The Blue's Clues display went down!

<Hey! Don't mess with Blue!> Cassie yelled, racing toward him.

<Sorry. I didn't know.>

<I have a niece who thinks Steve and Blue are the sun and the moon.>

<Cool. How about Intermediate Series?> He rested a ham-sized fist on a rack, preparing to push it over.

<Just get out of the kids' section, Marco,> Cassie warned. <What's the matter with you? Go up front and trash the computer magazines or something. Man, I hate this. Bookstores are like church or something.>

I grabbed the edges of a six-by-six-foot table on which were piled seriously discounted books and —

WHOOMMPPFF!

The Yeerk manager wailed in his corner.

Hundreds of oversized art books and fancy address books and biographies about some boy who was a star for about a minute went piling onto the floor.

"Look, Mommy!" I whipped around to see some little boy yanking on his mother's jeans and pointing at Marco. "It's Curious George!"

<Hey, little dude, I'm a gorilla. Curious George is a monkey. Lady, you should buy your kid an encyclopedia!> Marco picked up a slightly smashed box from the floor. <How about investing in a CD-

47

ROM version? *Zillions* magazine, the *Consumer Report*, for kids' rates . . .>

"WAAAAAAH! Curious George is mean!"

The kid's mother dropped to her knees and threw her arms around her howling son.

<Oh, man. Sorry,> Marco said, sounding genuinely contrite. <I didn't mean to scare him.>

<We have been here for four of your minutes,> Ax announced calmly.

I lumbered over to the Controller manager. Reached down and wrapped him in a bear hug. I squeezed him tight, crushing the air from his lungs. His face was inches from my muzzle. He was shaking and gasping for air.

I squeezed harder. Harder till the veins in his neck stood out.

<We know you, Yeerk. All of you. There's no safety anymore.>

His face was turning blue.

<There's no place to hide. You tell Visser Three that. You tell him we've only just begun. You tell him it's time to go home.>

"Next stop, Style-a-riffic!"

"What's that?"

Cassie, of course.

<Style-a-riffic is a place where women . . .>

"And men," I pointed out.

Ax inclined his head. <Where humans go to have their hair cut, teased, treated with chemicals, or tortured into an updo. Liquid acrylic is applied to the delicate human fingernail and dried in a cancer-causing machine much like your microwave. Hair from above the eyes is torn out by the roots. Skin from the feet is sliced off with sharp metal instruments. Hair from the legs, however . . .>

49

Cassie held up a hand. "I get the picture, Ax."

"TV commercial?" Marco guessed and Ax nodded.

"So, why Style-a-riffic?" Cassie asked. "What's the Yeerk connection?"

"First, it's the largest beauty salon in town," I said. "Second, Tobias learned that Mrs. Chapman is their best client — and co-owner. You tell me there's not a Yeerk running the place."

"You're enjoying this, aren't you?" Marco asked me.

"Yeah. I am. We've taken it and taken it, and barely fought back. Now they're scared. And they'll be more scared, soon. Should have done this a long time ago."

"Yeah, well, we didn't have the mighty Warrior Princess in charge before," Marco said.

I heard the tone of sarcasm. But I didn't care. *That's right,* I thought, *but now I am in charge, and now the Yeerks are going to pay.*

Jake would be proud of me when he got back. Or maybe a little jealous. Maybe even a lot jealous. That was okay, too. Things changed. People changed. Situations changed. Jake had been the leader for a long time. Maybe it was time he took a well-deserved rest.

Again, we struck. Quick and unexpected as lightning.

"Ahhh!"

"Ohhh!"

"Eeek!"

<Oh, yeah, this is a beauty salon,> Marco said. <"Eeek"? What am I, a mouse?>

This time, we came in through the front door. The bored, airhead receptionist didn't even look up.

"Do you have an appointment?" she said, cracking a piece of smelly, grape-flavored bubble gum.

And then she looked up. And then she fainted.

CLUNK! Facedown on the desk. It was pretty funny. Plus, she used way too much hairspray.

<Let's do it!>

Then we hit the nearest sporting goods store. CRAASSSHHH!

BOOMPP. BOOMPP. BOOMPPBOOMPPBOO-MPP.

An entire wire container, six feet high, crammed with basketballs, hit the floor!

<Hey, I like these Skechers . . .>

<Put 'em down, Marco!>

"Aaahhh! What are you doing to my store!" Tasset. Owner of All That! Sporting Goods. Controller.

Cassie. Chewing through the mesh on a tennis racket. <This had better not be catgut is all I'm saying,> she growled.

Tobias, using talons and beak to deflate rubber rafts and rowboats suspended from the ceiling.

FWAPP!

Ax, smashing glass cases full of sports watches with well-aimed blows of his blade.

Announcing, <It is time.>

SCREEEEEPPPP! EEERRREEEPPP!

The metal bars of the gate separating the safety deposit boxes from the rest of the bank just kind of — fell apart in my paws.

<They don't make gates the way they used to,> I commented.

BONK!

The armed guard was down. Something about the sight of a grizzly and gorilla playing with metal made him knock himself in the head with his own nightstick.

<You know, after this experience, I'm thinking that putting my money under the mattress is not such a bad idea.>

<What money? Like you have any money!> I taunted.

<Some of us save our allowance,> Marco shot back, dragging the felled guard across the marble-floored room and propping him into an armchair. <Some of us don't run right out and spend it all at The Gap.>

Cassie had herded the bank customers into a small office and stood outside, growling menacingly, barring the closed door.

"Ah! Help! Somebody, call the police! Ask for Sergeant . . ."

It was the Yeerk-controlled bank manager, Mr. Arundel.

Arms in the air, navy blue suit and yellow power tie askew. Shouting to be heard through the door of the closed office.

FWAPP!

Ax, coming up from behind the panicked bank manager, smacking his head with the side of his tail blade.

Mr. Arthur Arundel, down for the count. Unable to call out the name of a Controller cop.

A cop who'd no doubt know exactly how to deal with the Andalite bandits. By alerting Visser Three.

<Rachel, we should bail,> Tobias said, flapping up from a desktop he'd been ravaging.

<But it hasn't been four minutes yet!>

<Someone's probably already tripped the silent police alarm.>

<Okay, okay,> I grumbled. <Let's go!>

<Was that Chapman going into that cigar store?>

<Doesn't he know smoking is bad for him?>

Tinkletinkletinkletinkle!

53

The plate glass window was gone!

I shook a few shards out of my shaggy brown fur and stepped up into the tobacconist's shop.

CRUNCH! Glass compacted beneath my feet. Whatever.

Tobias soared in after me, flared, pulled up, and dove for Assistant Principal Chapman.

"Tseeer!"

"Aaah!"

Chapman swatted at the red-tailed hawk menacing him.

Big mistake.

"Ow!"

Chapman fell back into an overstuffed armchair, the kind Bruce Wayne and rich old men in smoking jackets are supposed to laze around in. Lines of bright red blood trickled down his cheeks.

The owner bent and grabbed something from behind a counter.

<No you don't.> Marco none too gently removed the thirty-eight special from the man's shaking hand. <Smoking and playing with loaded weapons? Tsk, tsk.>

BONK!

The guy went down, the impression of a gorilla fist plastered on his face.

Cassie butted at a wooden Indian until it toppled, destroying a glass case of silver cigar cutters and pocket-sized leather carrying cases. <Later for that thing,> she muttered.

I loomed above Chapman and delivered the same message I had been delivering all day.

<It's over for you,> I said. <Go home, Yeerk. Go home.>

<It is time,> said Ax, proclaiming our job was done. Again.

CHAPTER 10

We ruled! The old standbys — force and surprise — served us well. Put us totally in charge of the town!

I was pumped! Psyched! This was my plan and I was in charge and we were kicking butt in the spectacular way I knew we would.

Hard to believe I'd ever doubted myself, even for a moment.

Hard to believe that even for a minute I'd questioned my ability to rule, lead, direct. Make tough decisions in the depths of crisis. Exploit my soldiers' particular talents.

I was made to be leader! Hero, warrior, king. I'd known that all along. Character is destiny. . . .

After the cigar store we hit Fred's Fitness Center on Peach Street downtown, where at least two of the most popular trainers were Controllers. Maybe some day Kirk and Kristen will get over the embarrassment of Ax's slicing off their gym shorts in front of their worshipful yuppie clients. Maybe.

Two blocks away, we rampaged through Kinko's. The manager was a kid I recognized from around. He went to the local high school now. A seven-teen-year-old loser who'd joined The Sharing to get a life.

What he'd gotten was a Yeerk in his head. And now he was Mr. Career Path and all, Mr. Re-sponsibility, Mr. Self-Importance in a pathetic short-sleeved white dress shirt and clip-on tie. Please.

I thought it might be interesting to make a photocopy of his butt. Send it to his boss. Tack a second copy up on the break room bulletin board.

So I did.

While the others trashed the stock and ripped the insides out of expensive laser jet machines or whatever. Oh, yeah. Ax did something not nice to the rent-by-the-hour computers.

Then, it was on to the big law firm with three names. All three names were head honchos on the Yeerk payroll.

File cabinets do not stay intact when thrown from a tenth-floor window. Neither do water coolers.

Next, we paid a little visit to the chambers of Judge Forensik, in the private, secure area of the courthouse where judges have their offices. I remembered the judge from when we'd paid a visit to the Yeerk pool during the instant oatmeal episode.

Judge Sally Forensik was, on most occasions, a distinguished-looking older woman. On this particular afternoon, bawling and crawling under her big maple desk, black robes hiked around her knees, she didn't look terribly deserving of respect.

Just before we got out, Ax sliced the judge's massive desk into several smaller desks, one for each of her underpaid, overworked staff. Now that was an act of true justice.

We avoided The Gap and its concealed entrance to the Yeerk pool. Way too crowded with civilians, Tobias pointed out. Secretly, I was pleased. I wasn't thrilled about messing up good clothes.

We avoided the police station. Too many guns. Even I knew it would be too easy to get killed. And none of us wanted the accidental death of a real, hardworking human cop on our hands. It had been hard enough to avoid hurting the guards at the courthouse.

All day we raided and rampaged and put the fear into human-Controllers. Sustained minimal injuries. Made Visser Three look bad. Hoped the inspector was taking note. Hoped he was getting the message: Visser Three had accomplished nothing on Earth. We could hit him anywhere, any time.

<Go home, Yeerk. Earth will never be yours.>

After the raid on Phil's Hardware, we split up. Left Controller Phil bound head to toe in two rolls of silver duct tape. Planned to meet in a half hour at the highly hyped Community Center the Yeerks had recently opened.

The Community Center was the scene of one of our most dangerous missions — find and destroy the Anti-Morphing Ray. A mission Tobias would never — could never — forget. One he'd never purge from his memory, from the hawk or human or mysteriously Andalite part of him.

During that mission Tobias had been a voluntary POW. An act of supreme sacrifice and bravery. The experience had almost destroyed him. It had scared me to death.

I had wanted more than anything to destroy his torturer. I'd spared her life once, at Tobias's request.

I guess Tobias is a better person than me.

Anyway, bad, haunting memories didn't mean we could stay away from this center of Yeerk activity. Especially now. I figured we'd find a whole bunch of high-ranking Controllers gathering there to panic and plan. Maybe even the visser himself. No doubt he'd been contacted by now, told about the total chaos the Andalite bandits were causing.

It was a dangerous place to attack — so many Controllers in a concentrated area. And here they would have Hork-Bajir shock troops. A very different proposition from scaring off civilians and roughing up human-Controllers. I wasn't sure exactly what we'd do once we got there.

But I knew I'd figure out something. I was Rachel! Hero warrior and interim king!

Tobias flew ahead to do what reconnaissance he could.

Marco took off with Ax, in human morph, right behind him.

Cassie and I walked a few blocks uptown. Once we were sure we weren't being followed, we'd morph to birds in a filthy but very private alley we'd spotted earlier.

There was a bounce in my step. I felt like howling and laughing and leaping up onto a sign-post and twirling in midair! Like Gene Kelly in that old movie *Singing in the Rain.*

There was chaos in the streets!

Maybe not chaos but there was definitely confusion. At least there was evidence of something going on.

Lots of police cars, just kind of cruising along.

Shopkeepers shutting down before usual closing time.

Clusters of people talking hurriedly, glancing over their shoulders nervously. Anticipating the next bizarro attack.

"Boo!"

The two men in suits flinched as Cassie and I passed.

"Jeez, Rachel, could you not call attention to us, please," Cassie muttered. "We all split up for a reason."

We passed a home electronics store. You know, stereos, beepers, cell phones, TVs.

One of the TVs in the window was tuned to the local news station. Well, to the temporary live-feed the station had hooked up after this morning's raid.

"Look! She's talking about us!" I grabbed Cassie's arm and pulled her closer to the window. We couldn't hear the announcer's voice, but the shots of the wrecked TV studio were clear enough.

"C'mon, Rachel," Cassie said. "We can watch a report later. Right now, we've got to move."

I shrugged off Cassie's hand. "Just wait a

minute, okay? I want to see if they show us tearing up the place!"

They did. Just a few grainy flashes as cameras tumbled and then nothing as cameras broke.

And then they showed something else. Across the bottom of the screen, in medium, white letters. The words:

One man dead in attack on WKVT. Visiting his grandson from Kansas, heart disease patient succumbs.

My own heart stopped. No. No.

Oh, God. No.

CHAPTER 11

We met up in part of the dense wood sur-rounding the Community Center and its play-ground and picnic areas. Still in our traveling bird morphs, mostly for security. Scattered on perches within several yards of one another.

<Tell them, Rachel> Cassie said, in private thought-speak. <If you don't, I will. But it should come from you.>

<I know, I know,> I growled. <I know.>

Marco narrowed his osprey eyes and looked from me to Cassie.

Ax, as northern harrier, was barely visible from my perch.

Tobias . . .

<That old man,> I blurted. <From the TV stu-

63

dio this morning. The one Tobias saw fall. He died.>

<It was a heart attack,> Cassie added gently. <That's all we know.>

Silence.

<Well, that's nice,> Marco said finally. <That's just beautiful.>

<The man's death is unfortunate. Perhaps it was even avoidable. But there is nothing we can do to change the fact of it.> Ax. Of course.

<Tobias?>

I was glad Cassie spoke to him. I wasn't sure I could. I felt — uncomfortable.

He'd seen potential trouble. He'd told me to get us out of the studio. I'd said no. I'd been having too good a time.

<All clear so far,> he reported from the high oak branch on which he perched as our most experienced lookout.

He didn't comment on the old man. He didn't even look at me. Or say he was sorry — for me.

<Look,> I said, suddenly angry, <it wasn't my fault. We all agreed to do this mission. Nobody forced anybody. We all agreed: Hit them hard, scare them, attack, attack, attack. I'm sorry the guy died but . . .>

<Rachel.> Cassie cut me off. <Nobody's saying it's your fault.>

<It's what they're not saying,> I muttered.

And then I felt even angrier. We were doing a good job so far!

And I was the leader! It was my place to keep us doing a good job. My duty.

No one could ever blame me for not doing my duty. <You know what?> I went on. <The Yeerks are spooked. We've got them right where we want them.>

<Good. Great. Mission accomplished!> Marco snapped.

<No. Not yet. Okay, there's only a handful of people in the picnic area. Maybe a Sharing subcommittee or maybe recruits, not Controllers yet. Either way, they're no real threat to us outside the building. Tobias, what's going on inside?>

He turned his intense hawk glare on me. For a moment. <There's some kind of meeting going on in a small, ground floor room at the back. Lots of very grim-looking Controllers. Some look more ticked off than scared. Some look really scared.>

<Any sign of the visser?> Marco asked.

<No. Doesn't mean he's not in the building,> Tobias said.

<It also doesn't mean he's not in morph as one of the humans in that room,> Cassie pointed out. <Or in some other morph.>

<We need more information. There could be Hork-Bajir on the premises, hiding, waiting for

an attack,> Ax added. <There could be the inspector.>

Tobias fluttered and resettled his wings. <They'll be expecting us. Some kind of intrusion, at least. We're not a surprise by now. We have to be careful.>

<I'm not sure this attack is even necessary,> Marco added. <I mean, we got the point across, right? Okay, Animorphs rule. Let's leave it at that before some other innocent bystander gets croaked.>

<Let Jake take it from here, when he gets back day after tomorrow,> Cassie suggested.

<I don't believe this!> I cried. <This is not the time to quit! This is not the time to get all nervous! We break in and we kick butt. We stick with the plan!>

<All right,> Marco said calmly. <I'll go in. But only after infiltration. Only when we know what we're getting into. Only if we think we have a reasonable chance of getting out.>

<I agree with Marco.>

<You, too, Cassie?> I wished I were human so I could make a sound of disgust. <You people kill me. Every attack so far has been a success. And you want to blow it now? By the time we check out the building the meeting could break up and everyone could be gone! What then?>

<Rachel —>

<No. No one says "no" to Jake,> I challenged. <Suddenly, I'm leader so it's okay to be all rebellious and mutiny? I don't think so. You chose me as leader. I got us through today okay. Didn't I? Didn't I?>

Another weird silence. Did Jake have to deal with these weird silences?

<She's right,> Tobias said. <We chose her.>

More silence. At least no one turned or flew away.

<Look,> I said, the inevitable prebattle excitement building in spite of the lack of enthusiasm and support the others were showing. <This is going to be fantastic. The last raid of the day. We'll leave the Yeerks with an experience they'll never forget.>

I looked around my wary group of feathered warriors. Imagined a hugely grinning, glittery eyed, adrenaline-soaked look on my own human face. And said, <If you guys are really that worried, we'll go in with maximum firepower. We all go in as polar bears!>

CHAPTER 12

"Did I hear you correctly?" Marco, almost totally demorphed, cupped his hand to his ear. "'Cause I don't see anything wrong with our usual battle morphs."

"He's got a point, Rachel." Cassie, now also human, stood next to him on the fragrant, pine-needle-covered ground, still hidden in the woods. "We know our morphs. They've been working for us all day. We handle them best."

"We're going for mass here, people," I said, pushing down the defensiveness I knew was creeping into my voice. They were still arguing with me! "Bulk. Spectacle. Going out in style. Besides, we want to send the message that there are a lot of us."

I knew I was right. I *knew* it.

So I waited and felt every muscle in my face tighten. Harden. No expression. Give them nothing but determined, fearless leader. Hero. Warrior. King.

No objections.

Not from Marco or Cassie or Ax. Not even from Tobias.

"Then, let's do it," I said, finally.

Morphing isn't pretty. It's not rational or logical or predictable.

And it's uncomfortable.

Though the idea is worse than the reality. Skin pinching and withering. Organs smooshing or stretching. Bones scraping together or being hollowed out. Huge, bulky muscles slapped on a narrow skeleton not yet ready for them.

Not exactly fun to think about but once the process gets going, it's bearable. Especially when you're not morphing something gross like a fly.

This time, the first thing to change was . . .

WHUMPPFFH! WHUMPPFFH!

I was down on my two front paws. Each a foot across, round, distributing my weight like snowshoes. Five toes and five thick claws. Good for traction. And for grabbing prey.

My back legs, heavy, stocky, shot out from the expanding round of whitish hair that was my middle.

My shoulders bulged. My butt exploded out. Two hundred. Six hundred. One thousand. Fifteen hundred pounds of blubber and muscle and fur before I reached my full bulk!

I was a fifteen-hundred-pound arctic beast, largest land carnivore — from the shoulders down.

<Whoa,> Marco said, his own morph complete but for still-sprouting hair. <You look like someone in one of those costumes with the big, detachable head. The kind that walk around amusement parks, terrifying little kids. Except you're missing the head.>

"Yeah, thanks. I hadn't notifff . . ."

And then, finally, my head began to shift and reshape. From an almost circle to an almost oblong. Pinkish skin turned black and sprouted the whitish, hollow tubes that are the polar bear's hairs. Miniature greenhouses, conducting warmth to my heat-absorbing black skin.

My eyes stayed pretty much where they were, facing forward. Sight was about the same. Better than my grizzly morph. Hearing? No big deal.

But smell! Now that was amazing. Smells meant food. And food meant . . .

Meat. Close by. Only just beyond that concrete-and-brick wall. No problem.

<So, think they picked up Mickey D's on the way in?> Marco, now fully polar bear, swung his

70

football-shaped head from side to side, inhaling through his smallish black nose.

<You know, I think I smell a Filet-O-Fish.> said Cassie. <I've always had a secret love of the Filet-O-Fish sandwich . . .>

<Perhaps the temporary inhabitants of this so-called Community Center will share their greasy fried flesh treats with us. . . .>

<Uh, people,> I said, myself fighting the polar bear's instinctive urge to feast. <Ax-man? Get a grip. This isn't the time for protein snacks.>

Tobias lumbered forward, each step like a human's, the heel of each massive paw touching the ground before the toes. <Remember, everyone,> he said blandly. <These are humans. Controllers, but humans all the same. We're here to scare them. Not to hurt. Or kill.>

I was stunned. He'd meant that for me! Me.

I didn't need his advice. His warnings.

I knew this was just another busting-up mission. I knew that!

All day long, at every raid, I'd been in control of myself. Of my morphs. I had! I hadn't been responsible for that old man's dying —

<So?> Marco said. <You gonna say it? Or am I?>

I hesitated. But only for a second. <Let's do it!>

"HHIISSSRRROOOAAARRRWWWW!"

71

CHAPTER 13

We were in!

Through the smallish back window, glass shattering, chunks of plaster flying. The wooden frame cracking and breaking.

One, two, three, four, five polar bears!

One after the other, hurtling into the room from above, half-falling, half-sliding down the wall, crashing down onto a handful of unsuspecting human-Controllers.

They screamed. Jumped from their seats. Ran for the door. One fainted. Another wet his pants.

Fine. Let them panic. They were going to get what they deserved.

A good butt-kicking.

It was easy. I smacked a raised chair out of a man's hand.

<That's for the old man,> I told him. I don't think he heard.

Marco barreled into a huddle of three Controllers and sent them scattering across the linoleum floor.

Ax and Cassie and Tobias rolled and rumbled and rampaged, bumping into one another's massive bulky bodies and knocking their heads against the low ceiling as they terrorized the Yeerk-infested humans. Tore the portable video screen off a wall. Threw a podium through a back window.

I laughed. At this rate, the attack would soon be over. We'd smash a few more skulls, break a few more pieces of furniture, and get out.

<Rachel! Hork-Bajir!> Tobias shouted.

I swung my massive body to face the interior door.

Yeerk shock troops. So what?

We could take them.

<Attack!> I cried. Adrenaline pumped harder through my veins and I leaped forward, teeth bared, claws extended.

My teeth tore at leathery Hork-Bajir flesh. Forty-two weapons in my mouth alone!

With my massive paws I batted and smacked

and ripped! At eight feet I stood taller than any of the Controllers in the room. Human or alien.

"HHIISSSRRROOOAAARRRWWW!"

I shoved a human-Controller aside and watched as his head bounced off the edge of a small table. He slid, unconscious, to the floor.

To my right, Cassie smashed the head of one human-Controller against the head of another. Like something out of an old Three Stooges.

To my left, Marco and Tobias wrestled a Hork-Bajir to the ground. Where he stayed.

In front of me, Ax hurled a bleeding Hork-Bajir aside and smacked the pathetic little knife out of the hand of a human-Controller.

We were winning!

We would destroy this room and its Yeerk inhabitants and get away before anyone could call for help.

Before anyone could understand the extraordinary force that had defeated them!

And then the inspector would have to believe that Visser Three was totally harassed and incompetent and . . .

<Rachel! Behind you!>

ZZZZZZZIIIIIIISSSPPP!

Blindingly fast! A blue blur . . .

The inspector. The Garatron. Had to be. Nothing else moved like that.

A blur and Marco's head jerked to one side. His knees buckled.

THWAP!

Marco was down, moaning.

<Jump him!> I ordered.

<Can't see him!> Cassie yelled.

Insane! Tobias threw his huge body at the inspector. At the point in space where the inspector had been. Less than a half second earlier.

Thunk!

Tobias was facedown on the floor.

The inspector circled and spun like a whirling dervish around Cassie. Jim Carrey in *The Mask*. The Tasmanian Devil in a whirlwind around Yosemite Sam. Futilely she slapped the empty air with her paw, over and over again.

<Cassie! Watch out!> I cried.

Too late!

Dizzy from trying to follow the inspector's swirling path, she couldn't react in time. Couldn't dodge the swinging bladed arm of the Hork-Bajir who loomed behind her.

<AAAAGGGHHH!>

She was down! The Hork-Bajir raised his arm to strike again, to slice the polar bear's already bleeding back.

Two down! No!

<No you don't, buddy.> Marco! Stumbling into

the Hork-Bajir from behind, buckling its knees, shoving it away from Cassie.

<OOOWWWRRR!>

I'd been hit!

Shot in the belly at close range by a human-Controller I hadn't seen sneaking up on me. I'd been too distracted by the inspector's infuriating speed and evasiveness.

This Yeerk-carrying human was going to pay for that! If only I could rear up on my hind legs . . .

ZZZIIISSSPPP!

THWAAAPP!

My head jerked violently to the left. I could hear the bones in my neck crack and creak.

Pathetically I raised one front leg — and stumbled to the ground.

The room spun! Bodies, human and alien. Flailing. Falling.

The flash of gunpowder. The clashing of blades.

The hissing growl of polar bears, growing weaker.

I had to get up, get back into battle!

Slowly, painfully, I raised my bruised head.

And saw the blue blur come to a dead stop about twenty feet in front of me. Speak to a blue deerlike creature with a bladed tail who stood just inside the door.

<Ihaveseenenough.Ileaveyoutocleanupthemess,mydearVisser.>

With an odd grace the inspector walked off through the door held open for him by a heavily bleeding human-Controller.

Lose one opponent. Gain another.

No way could we win against a dozen still-standing Hork-Bajir and twenty human-Controllers with guns. And Visser Three. In a space barely big enough to accommodate five polar bears standing still.

Exhaustion. I had never felt so drained and depleted. And the pain in my gut . . .

Maybe it was time to . . .

Pllaaaammmph!

CHAPTER 14

I swung my head around.

Fllooooommph!

The visser had begun to morph.

To some massive, horrible — thing.

From his proud Andalite body shot folds of gray skin. Flaps of stinking flesh, piling on top of one another, layer upon layer. Like pudding dumped from a bowl.

Skin like buckets of quicksand slapped onto a six-, seven-, eight-foot monster!

Eyes like tiny rotted raisins. Arms and legs like columns of poured mud, two feet around.

A stomach that roiled out like a wave and slapped onto the floor!

That kept on growing!

78

Skin that oozed an outrageously foul stench. Think sewer. Then corpse.

What little air there was in that small over-crowded room was already stale with the odors of sweat and blood. Boiling with the heat of so many bodies. The visser's reeking morph made breathing almost impossible.

And the heat!

My body felt bloated with it. My skin stretched over layers of dense blubber. My fur coat felt like the heavy lead blanket the doctor drapes over you before pointing an X-ray machine at your chest.

Oppressive!

Too late I realized the polar bear — an animal that expends twice the amount of energy at a given speed than any other mammal — an animal covered in layers of insulating blubber — was not the morph for this job.

<Too hot. Gotta . . . can't breathe.>

<And, uh, guys, I'm bleeding pretty bad,> said Tobias.

<Perhaps we should have chosen our usual battle morphs,> Ax said unnecessarily, his voice grim. <We are all one thing, with no flexibility. We must withdraw.>

<Yeah. Go for the window!> I shouted. <I'll hold off the visser. Go! Go!>

<Rachel, don't be crazy . . .>

<I said get out, Tobias! Now!>

I was vaguely aware of massive white shapes, splotched with gore, lumbering toward the outer wall. Dragging themselves over a pile of bloody Hork-Bajir. Warriors dead and dying.

"HHHSSSRRROOOAAARRWW!"

With all the willpower I could muster I reared up on my hind legs. My battered oblong head swung from side to side as I took a step closer to the visser's disgusting, still-growing monster.

I'd never survive an assault. Only one thing to do.

Attack!

I threw my suddenly puny body into the grotesque fleshy monster. Stumbled as I met little resistance against the reeking pulpy mass.

<Fool of an Andalite!> the visser laughed. <You have failed even to bruise the flesh of this admittedly foul creature. Your efforts to damage this body are futile!>

I pulled back. Again, threw myself against the pile of stinking gray flesh. Again. Again!

Until the visser reached down with one putrid claw and plucked my fifteen-hundred-pound body off his like a chimpanzee plucking a flea off its belly.

And with a wet spray of foul breath — tossed me against the far wall!

I smashed into the plaster and slid to the floor. My senses were dulled. Fire raced down my back and across my ribs. My front left paw was pulpy and red. But I wasn't dead.

And that's all that mattered.

The window! On the wall above me!

A quick glance around the destroyed room.

Marco, Ax, Cassie, Tobias.

I couldn't see any of them.

Good.

Just piles of Hork-Bajir and battered human-Controllers, groaning, struggling to their feet.

No inspector.

And Visser Three's outrageous morph slowly shrinking.

Time to bail.

I lumbered to my feet. My head spun with the effort. I felt a stream of blood flow down my forehead. And another jab of pain — awful! — down my back where my spine had crashed against the wall.

The window was about seven feet up the wall. The glass and frame had been smashed when we stormed the room.

With effort, I stood on my hind legs. Stepped onto the back of a felled Hork-Bajir. Reached. And with my last ounce of strength hauled my broken body up and across the torn sill.

And tumbled to the litter-strewn ground.

I was out!

We were safe!

<Marco! Ax! Tobias! Where's . . .>

I didn't finish the question.

Because the look on Marco's face, the set of Ax's shoulders, and the way Tobias turned away gave me my answer.

Cassie was still inside.

CHAPTER 15

<One hour and fifteen minutes. Seventy-five minutes, total.>

"This is just fabulous. This is just perfect!" Marco raged. "In less than two hours Cassie's going down. One way or the other. Infestation? Maybe. Torture? Why not. Life as a gigantic fur ball? Possible."

<Marco.> Tobias's voice was emotionless. <Stop. I'm sure Rachel feels bad enough . . .>

"And she should!" Marco whirled to glare at me.

I lowered my head and the tears spilled faster.

"Nice, Rachel," Marco spat. "The 'Don't-be-mean-to-me I'm-a-girl' thing is pathetic."

<Marco!> It was Ax. <That is enough. Unproductive. And enough.>

We were in Cassie's barn. Cassie's favorite place. Which, thanks to me, she might never see again.

"I . . . I thought she was out . . ." I whispered.

<We've got to deal with this situation,> Tobias went on. <If the Yeerks infest Cassie and force her to demorph, we're history. The mission is over. The entire war is over. It might be already.>

Marco snorted. "Shouldn't we let our new fearless leader decide the next move? She's been just fantastic with strategy so far. I, for one, am impressed."

I sniffed and swiped at my eyes with the back of my hand. "Marco . . ."

"Yes? Did you want to say something to me?" He crossed his arms and stared. "'Cause I don't know if a macho warrior like you wants to be talking to me. I'm the one who *thinks* too much. I'm the *boring* one with the *Hamlet complex*. The one who says, 'Gee, Rachel. Don't you think we should take a look first? Investigate? Prepare? You know, before we march into certain death?'"

Okay, now I was mad. I'd screwed up really, really badly. But wasn't I punishing myself enough? For God's sake, I was crying! Not something I made a habit of doing. "I didn't know that Garatron inspector would be there!" I shouted, my fists clenched.

Marco shook his head. Like he was disgusted. "Yeah, well, you would have if you'd listened to reason."

<We are wasting time,> Ax said. <The visser has probably taken Cassie to the Yeerk pool.> Ax still hadn't looked at me. Not right at me. Not once since we'd run off from the Community Center, flown back to the barn. <Our course is clear.>

Tobias stretched and refolded his wings. <Rachel's our leader, Ax. We might not be thrilled with that decision right now but we're the ones who made it. I think we should take responsibility for it. Stick with it.>

My stomach clenched. I felt chilled.

Not exactly a strong endorsement from Tobias.

But why *would* he be pleased with me? Why *should* he stick up for me? My show-off performance had put us all — all — in serious danger. Had quite possibly condemned us to death.

An old man, dead. Cassie . . .

I was going to be sick. I clapped my hand over my mouth.

No. Get control, Rachel. Not here. Not now.

"No!" I turned to Marco. Tobias. "Ax. Please. Look at me." He did, with his main eyes. "I'm not your leader. Not anymore. I can't bring that old man back to life. I can't tell you to go down to the Yeerk pool to rescue Cassie. I can't tell you to do anything! I screwed up. I . . ."

<Rachel. All leaders make mistakes on occasion. It is not a desirable thing but it is an observable truth. Tobias is correct. You are our leader. You must behave like a commanding officer.>

I shook my head. "No. Ax . . ." I swallowed hard and looked to Tobias. "And Tobias. Thanks for the loyalty. It must be hard, pretending to have faith in me. And Marco? Thanks for the honesty." I laughed a forced, sick laugh. "It's ugly but I deserve it. But . . . I'm going down to the Yeerk pool alone. It's the only way."

"Are you on medication?" Marco put his hands to his head. "No, I really want to know. Seriously. 'Cause I think your dosage needs to be adjusted."

"I'm going alone. That's final. Look, Cassie went down alone when she had to."

"When the rest of us were totally incapacitated," Marco shot back. "Different situation. She had no choice. You do."

<It would be suicidal,> Ax said. <I cannot imagine Prince Jake approving of such an action.>

"Yeah, well, Jake's not here," I snapped. Even to my own ears I sounded like a petulant child.

"And if he had been I guess none of this would have happened."

<So, it's Jake's fault?> Tobias said harshly. <That he trusted us to handle situations while he was away? That we chose you as interim leader? That you made a mistake and now want to bail on us? I don't know, Rachel. Maybe you really don't deserve to be leader.>

Tobias . . .

Guilt. Shame.

Overwhelming sadness. And anger.

Why was this happening? How could things have gotten so bad? Gone so wrong?

It was all too much. Too much!

I couldn't . . .

"I quit. I resign. Let Marco be leader," I yelled, kicking an old wooden crate against the wall. A wounded raccoon moaned nervously in its cage. "It's what he's wanted all along. I'm out of here."

CHAPTER 16

Marco followed me out of the barn.

"Rachel. Wait up."

I did. I don't know why.

But I threw my arms up in the air and slapped them down against my thighs and tossed back my head and growled.

He trotted up and came to stand in front of me.

"No," he said.

"What do you mean, 'no'? Don't want to have to deal with my mess?" I said flatly, brushing away a final tear and pretending it was a speck of dirt. "I understand that. It's a no-win situation. And you're nothing if not pragmatic, Marco."

Marco nodded. "You're right about that. Lousy odds for success. And I am pragmatic."

"The odds are always lousy. But Jake beats the odds."

"Yeah. We're lucky we have Jake. But he's screwed up, too."

"Your pity isn't really helping me, Marco."

"Jake never walks out. Never quits."

"Yeah, well, goody for Saint Jake. You're the one who didn't want me in charge. Why not just take your big victory and be happy. The Animorphs are all yours till the Almighty Jake comes home."

"Look, I can't lead. Not right now. This isn't my mission."

"Look, maybe someday I'll be in charge. If I am, I'll probably screw up. Like I said, even Saint Jake blows it sometimes. What makes you so special, anyway?"

"Yeah? Then it's your turn to screw up. I'm gone."

Marco grabbed my arm. I jerked it away. He looked as angry as I was.

"Listen to me, you mall-crawling psycho, we have one hour and ten minutes to get Cassie out of the Yeerk pool. Now, I can come up with a clever plan. I can work all the angles. I can see the perfect solution. But all that takes time. We don't have time, Rachel. We don't have time for clever and subtle. We need reckless. We need impulsive. We need dangerous. We need out-of-your-mind, pure adrenaline, butt-kicking, total out-there insanity."

He stabbed his finger in my face. "We could have used me, back at the Community Center. But right now we need you. We have an hour to save your best friend, Jake's girlfriend, and the entire human race. You got us into this, now get us out."

Tobias and Ax were still waiting in the barn.

I closed the door behind me. I stood just inside, Marco within arm's reach, peering into the blue-and-gray gloom of the barn.

It was evening, about six o'clock. I was already late for dinner but I'd deal with my mother's questions tomorrow. If she'd even noticed I was gone, with all the time she was spending at the office lately on a major new case.

"Tobias?" My voice came out a little raw. "We have to act. Now. Anything new we need to know about the entrances to the Yeerk pool?"

There was a beat of silence. I thought I saw Ax smile, in that incredible mouthless way Andalites smile. But I could have imagined that, too.

Another beat of silence. Tobias said, <What are you planning to —>

I slammed my fist into my other hand. "I'm planning to get Cassie out of there. Now answer my question. Everything you have on Yeerk pool entrances. *Now*."

<Gap dressing room. McDonald's bathroom. Community Center playground tunnel.>

"Any other options?" I asked quickly.

Tobias cocked his head and seemed to consider. <Possibly. There's a new office building a couple of blocks from the McQueen Building, where we were today. I've been watching it since it went up about two months ago. Strange thing is, it's still empty. No tenants.>

"Lousy real estate market?" Marco wondered.

<No. I watched the construction, too. Mostly it was kept under wraps, but nobody was expecting a hawk to be snooping around. I'm no engineer, but I'm pretty sure office buildings have things like stairwells and elevator shafts. But not this building. And I'm also pretty sure the roof is retractable.>

<Not a common feature of Earth dwellings, I believe,> Ax said.

<Right. The other day I thought I saw what had to be a cloaked Bug fighter dropping through the roof. I can't be sure. I was too far away, but you know, we've always wondered how the visser gets spacecraft in and out of the Yeerk pool. I don't —>

"Time check, Ax?"

<Sixty-five of your minutes.>

<I may be wrong about this place,> Tobias said.

"Take us half an hour to get there, another half hour to infiltrate," Marco said. "If it is a Yeerk cover, it'll be guarded. More so, now. Then, we'll need time to get to the Yeerk pool, find Cassie, bail out. I don't see it. Not in any sixty-five minutes."

"It doesn't take a Bug fighter that long," I said.

<We do not have a Bug fighter,> Ax said.

I took a deep breath. I had a terrible idea. A suicidal idea. I half smiled at Marco. "You wanted insane? I've got some insane."

CHAPTER 17

"Okay, Rachel. This *is* insane. I mean, genuinely insane. How are we going to get to that plane without getting shot at or eaten by German shepherds?"

Okay, so the situation looked a little grim. Morgan Airport. For small jets, both corporate and privately owned. Even though the sun hadn't yet set, too-bright white lights illuminated the airfield, which meant no convenient shadows in which to lurk. Flat, open terrain, which meant no natural cover.

High fences. Some of which just might deliver a nasty shock to anyone attempting to scale them. And if a jolt of electricity didn't get the intruder, rows of barbed wire would. That or one of the eighty-pound, highly trained guard dogs.

Human guards posted at every gate. Guns in low-slung holsters at their waists but lazy-looking, and wearing sunglasses — behind which they were probably dozing. But I was through making risky assumptions. At least, for the moment.

All these safety measures to protect the private jets of the rich and famous. And we were about to hijack one of them. I wondered if the owners had insurance. And then I spotted the corporate logo on the jet we'd targeted. And on the one next to it.

Philip Morris. Oh, yeah. The owners of these babies had insurance. Lots of it.

I shrugged. "No time. Ticktock. Back to basics: We make a run for it."

"I so knew you were going to say that." Marco turned to Ax and Tobias. "I knew she was going to say that."

"On the count of three, guys. One. Two. THREE!"

We were off!

Scrambling up the first fence, fingers grasping, sneakers jamming into then out of too-small toeholds. No electric jolt but plenty of barbed wire at the top. Launching ourselves over the prickly coils and dropping to the ground on the other side.

"Owowow!" Good thing we'd worn jeans and sweatshirts — stuff we'd stashed in Cassie's barn for emergencies — against the cool night air.

Across the concrete apron! Running full out! Weird to be running as a human. It had been a long time.

"Hey! You kids! Stop!"

"ROWROWROWROW!"

I glanced over my shoulder to see two German shepherds being held by their collars, straining to do what they were trained to do.

Take down the intruders!

I raced on. Our sneakers slapped the ground like hands clapping too fast and too loud.

A bullhorn now. "I said, stop in the name of the law! Or I'll let the dogs go!"

"Anyone got any liver snacks?" Marco panted. "Nice doggies!"

"Almost there! C'mon!"

I reached out desperately for the handrail of the retractable staircase and yanked myself up the first few steps.

A mechanic appeared underneath me, vacuum-type tool in hand. He must have come from under the plane.

"Hey, girlie! You can't . . ."

I darted a look at his balding head.

"Oh, yeah. I can."

He reached up and over the rail to grab me. I

twisted and he missed. I ran on and reached the door of the plane, Marco, Tobias, and Ax right behind me.

"ROWROWROWROW!"

"In, in in!" I shouted, dragging Ax — who'd had some trouble with the stairs — through the narrow opening.

Began to haul the stairs and door shut . . .

SLAM!

"Thank you, Rachel. Human legs are far too wobbly . . ."

"Later, Ax. Keep an eye on the guards."

"I could get used to this," Marco said, looking around the posh interior of the jet. "Not a problem. Cushy leather seats. Twelve-inch video monitors. Gorgeous women serving . . . hey, where *are* the babes?"

"Down, boy," I snapped. "Tobias, make sure the door is secured. Tight. Ax, can you fly this thing?"

"Without a doubt. But first I will demorph in preparation for throwing myself out at the appropriate time . . ."

"If not sooner," Marco muttered.

I growled. "You guys are not helping."

"I am," Marco said suddenly, turning from a window on the far side of the plane. "I'm telling you there's about, oh, ten guys with guns and nightsticks, ready to beat the crap out of us. Once they shoot their way inside, of course."

<I am ready, Prince — well, I am ready.>

Ax stood in the small cockpit, four legs braced firmly, and began to flip switches on the control panel with his nimble fingers.

MMMrrrr . . .

The engines came to life. Ax pushed a control stick forward slowly and the plane began to taxi.

"You sure you understand the concept of take-off, Ax-man?" Marco asked nervously.

Ax swiveled his stalk eyes and gave Marco a look of disdain. <I imagine that I will be able to comprehend this highly sophisticated human technology,> he said dryly.

The jet picked up speed. Ax steered it onto the taxiway and turned toward the runway. But still, it felt like we were crawling!

"Ax! The guards are gaining on us! Can't you . . ."

Ax turned onto the runway and opened up the throttle. At last, some speed!

Suddenly . . .<Ax! Look out!>

A deer! It had bounded out of the woods off to the right! Too fast, too close for Ax to stop!

The deer froze twenty yards in front of us, its eyes glowing in the night, stunned by the jet's headlights, oblivious to the shouts of men and the frantic barking of dogs!

97

Szwoooosh . . .

Ax swerved off the runway and the jet trundled over the grassy field. It missed the deer by — feet! Inches, it seemed!

"Excellent save, Ax!" I cried as he guided the plane back onto the concrete.

<Thank you, Rachel,> he said, his voice tight. <But I am afraid that evasive tactic cost us the necessary speed required to get the jet off the ground by the end of the runway.>

<They're getting real close,> Tobias warned. <And they've got a security van.> He had demorphed and was perched on the back of one of the two forward-facing passenger seats.

"Is there any chance, Ax?" I shouted.

<There is a small chance I can get us up. But if I fail . . .>

I darted a quick glance at Marco and Tobias.

Marco nodded, his eyes dark.

Tobias . . . his inscrutable hawk stare was unchanged, but I knew.

"Do it, Ax! Go for it!"

Faster, faster, faster. The engines louder. Trees rushing by, blurring . . .

I gripped the back of the pilot's seat, my knuckles white.

Yes!

<We have liftoff,> Ax said calmly.

I ran a hand over my forehead, beaded with

sweat. I was nervous. Excited. Thankful. The rescue mission was underway.

We rose. Gained altitude and speed. Higher. Faster. Over the anonymous country, suburb, and city where we live. Toward the new Beane Tower. And the Yeerk pool. And Cassie.

CHAPTER 18

Higher. Higher. And faster.

The sky slowly darkening, the blue deepening.

My heart pounding in my chest. Counting every beat as a second in time.

Ticktock.

Cassie's time running out.

Our time running out!

Finally — finally! We were at seven thousand feet in the air over the Beane Tower.

"Ready, Ax?" I asked.

<We are in position.>

"Everybody ready? Marco, start your morph."

"I've changed my mind," he said. "All that

stuff I said about needing insane? I was just suffering from low blood sugar."

"Marco. Do it."

<It is time,> Ax said. <Do you recall the in­structions I gave you?>

"Yeah," I said. "Get on with it."

Szwooooosh . . .

"Holy . . ."

A ninety-degree dive! Nose down, hurtling straight for the roof of the Beane Tower!

A roof that looked pretty seriously solid right now.

"Okay, Ax! Give me the stick!" I shouted over the roar of the engines and rushing wind. "Morph! Then the three of you bail!"

<Rachel . . .>

"It's okay, Tobias," I said. "I'll be okay."

Ax dropped to his knees and dug his weak Andalite fingers as far into the nap of the plane's carpeting as they would go. With weak Andalite arms he strained to pull his heavy body up to the door. With stronger, more muscled legs he shuffled up and forward.

Struggling to keep from falling back, Ax pulled open the door and barely caught himself as the suck of air rushed from the jet.

I struggled to hold the controls steady until the others got out. To keep my body from being forced from the seat by the ferocious vacuum. To keep from smashing headfirst down against the windshield.

I was vaguely aware of Ax shrinking to northern harrier. And an osprey and a red-tailed hawk giving themselves up to the enormous sucking power of the wind, and letting themselves float out of the plane.

Then, finally, was brutally aware of being alone in a four-ton jet, plummeting through the air toward what still looked like a too, too solid object.

Did I really expect the roof to retract for me? The enemy?

Had to ride the jet down. Ax was clear about that. Autopilot would be useless. Had to wait, wait, till that rectangular roof seemed to fill my entire field of vision, till there was no way to miss, till . . .

Morph! Now!

Bald eagle.

As soon as I thought it, I released my grip on the arms of the pilot's seat.

SMASH!

I had braced myself but I was still thrown into the wall, then a passenger seat.

SMASH!

I ignored the bruises and allowed myself to be pulled, yanked, dragged toward the open door.

Yes! I'd made it.

I let go my grip and my still-human body flew from the plane.

Insanity!

I watched through wind-battered, tearing eyes the jet seeming to slowly — then more quickly — drop away below me. Knew my friends had to be still above me, following. Engines still wide open. I felt the oven heat of the backwash.

Morph! Morph! Morph!

Head over heels! Heels that were shriveling, narrowing into the powerful, gripping talons of the hunter.

Too slow!

Panic . . . *Fight it, Rachel! You're the hero, warrior king! You can do this. You have to do this!*

This is who you are.

<Rachel!>

Had someone called my name?

Hurtling, hurtling . . .

And then I felt the tickling along my arms, legs, back. The tickling that meant a tracery of feathers was etching itself on my skin. A tattoo that would cover my entire body and then . . . raise into three dimensions!

But a feathered human couldn't fly! A feathered human would crash-land . . .

BOOOOMM!

The jet hit!

It hit the roof of the Beane Tower and plowed through the roof that had not retracted.

The jet exploded on impact, tearing a massive hole through the roof.

Whooooosh!

A fireball! Of amazingly enormous proportions that I, half-morphed and falling, speeding through the air, could not fail to see, hear, feel.

Blast after blast of intense heat! The air around me shimmered like the surface of a clouded, rippling lake. Then black, acrid smoke billowed up from the Beane Tower.

And I was falling, falling into the inferno! A feathered human now with the eagle's keen eyes. Better to see my own destruction rising up to meet me . . .

"Ahhhhhhhh!"

Had I cried out? Or had I screamed in my head? And what did it matter?

The shattered roof, so close! Jagged pieces of metal and broken glass, sticking up at crazy angles. All around the edge of the hole. Like ragged, dangerous teeth, ringing the gaping maw of a beast.

The flames!

Still morphing . . . Was I lighter? Had my bones hollowed?

The speed, the heat, the wreckage, the . . .

<Ahhhhhhh!>

ZWHOOOP!

I was through!

Sucked through the awful hole that had been the roof! Drawn down in the wake of the plummeting, fiery jet.

Feathers singed, lungs filled with smoke, but alive!

Morph, Rachel! Finish the morph!

Too fast! I was falling too fast! I'd smash into the jet, twisting and diving below me.

Be the eagle!

Down, down through one, two, three stories of empty building!

Tobias was right. No tenants. No floors or dividing walls or elevator shafts or staircases, either.

Just a hollow tube. A tunnel down to the . . .

Four, five, six stories!

Yes! Wings! My body still too large, not fully the eagle's yet, but . . .

I flapped, pulled up against the sucking wake of the plummeting jet, struggled . . .

Seven, eight stories!

<Ahhhhhh!>

BOOM!

CHAPTER 19

BABOOOM!

The wreckage of the jet crashed through a ceiling or a hatch or something.

I followed.

<Aaaahhh!>

Down through the opening! The plane falling, spiraling down from the high-domed roof of the Yeerk pool!

Through the thunderous rushing of sound that accompanied the hurtling jet I could make out the harrowing cries of involuntary hosts. A cry far too familiar.

"GHAFRASH! WATCH OUT!"

Could hear the stunned, panicked shouts of Hork-Bajir-Controllers. Could see them, barely, herding hosts back and away from the edge of the lead-colored pool itself. Away from the jet . . .

SPLOOOOSSHHH! SZZZZZZZZZ!

Into the pool! The still-flaming body of the jet tearing through the dull gray surface of the Yeerk pool. Disappearing for a moment.

The contents of the pool sizzling and sloshing and churning. Spitting up pieces of twisted metal that bobbed to the slimy, fiery surface.

Hundreds, maybe thousands of Yeerks were in that pool! How many were dead? How many had just been killed?

Pull up, Rachel! Pull up!

I flared, talons forward, killing airspeed.

Yes! I was fully eagle now.

I righted myself. Flapped and soared above the panic on the floor of the massive underground complex. No one seemed to notice an Earth bird in the commotion.

Involuntary hosts were being slammed into cages. Voluntary hosts, whose Yeerks were currently in the cauldron that was the Yeerk pool, were being slammed in alongside their reluctant brothers and sisters. Just in case.

But where was Cassie? My keen eagle eyes darted from right to left. I flapped higher, scoping the pool, the buildings . . . the two steel infestation piers.

And found her. A massive off-white beast, her

fur matted and stained with blood and gore. Her head hanging low. Each tree-trunk leg manacled to the other. Surrounded by three Hork-Bajir guards, one who held a blade to her throat.

No time to lose! Even with the Yeerk pool disrupted, Visser Three would demand the Andalite bandit be forcibly infested by a Yeerk. Forced to demorph. Compelled to reveal everything . . .

How many minutes did Cassie have left in morph?

I'd lost track. Fifteen? Five?

No time to look for the others! Had they even made it alive through the burning, jagged hole that was once the roof? Had they survived the flames and blasts of intense heat and . . .

<Cassie! It's me. Hang on!>

Only a slight, slight movement of her bent head. Enough for my keen eagle's eyes to detect. Not enough to give warning to her Hork-Bajir guards.

A surprise attack!

One bald eagle against who knew how many Yeerk warriors!

Adrenaline surged through my body and mind and soul.

It was insane.

It was necessary!

I dove. Flared, talons out. In for the kill!

Swooosh!

"Raaahhh!"

I tore at the eyes of the guard who held his bladed wrist at Cassie's neck. Immediately he dropped to his knees, blood dripping through the hands he'd raised to his face.

<Rachel!>

Attack! Talons extended, again. Another Hork-Bajir down. One more to go.

What was she . . .

Brilliant! Cassie was slowly, carefully demorphing. Controlling the demorphing process like only Cassie can. Shrinking, just enough to slip the manacles and chains that bound and incapacitated her.

Yanking the restraints away from her hind paws, tossing part into the still-roiling Yeerk pool. Wrapping another part partially around a front paw.

Now she was reversing the morph. Lumbering to her full height! Eight feet of towering polar bear! Powerful beyond imagining. And angry.

Cassie swung the heavy chain around her head. "HSSSSROOOAAARRR!"

Yes!

THWUUMP!

The third Hork-Bajir, stumbling to his feet after surviving my attack, was down.

Cassie fell to her four paws. I landed on her broad, strong back.

<Surprised to see me?> I asked.

<Sky falling in, flames everywhere, Yeerks running for cover? Who else would it be but you?>

Down the infestation pier, big taloned feet thudding and thundering, blades hissing as they slid and jostled against one another, came five Hork-Bajir.

SWAAAP! SWAAAP!

The bleeding, blinded Hork-Bajir were slammed out of their way.

<What's the plan, Rachel?>

<Stop them. Somehow.>

Closer! Then the Hork-Bajir leading the five guards slowed. Just a bit. Another few yards or so and all they'd need to do was push us back, off the pier, into the Yeerk pool. Easy. Why rush?

<Take off, Rachel!> Cassie said wildly. <Get out. I'll fight them off as best I can.>

<And then what? Less than ten minutes in morph, Cassie,> I guessed. <Then you're Nanook for life. No. I'm getting out of here and I'm taking you with me. We're barreling through. We charge for an exit.>

If they take anyone, I thought, *I'll make them take me. And then, I'll do whatever I have to do. Whatever.*

But now . . .

Almost within arm's reach!

I tensed for action. Beneath my talons I felt Cassie's muscles bunch and coil, ready to charge.

The lead Hork-Bajir guard raised his blade-wielding arm and . . .

<Halt!>

Thought-speak! Hugely loud. Thunderous. It could only belong to one person.

Visser Three.

The five Hork-Bajir stopped and stood as if frozen.

And then the horrible voice again.

<You are very lucky to be here today, Inspector. We have captured another Andalite traitor for your entertainment!>

CHAPTER 20

Not good.>

<No,> Cassie agreed.

CLOP CLOP CLOP CLOP.

The visser came into view at the far edge of the pool. Next to him — suddenly, as if by magic — appeared the inspector. That weird, spindly, faster-than-the-speed-of-sound creature. In some odd way, the cause of Cassie and me being trapped here.

Two blue-furred, four-legged aliens. Possibly related only by the fact that each was a slave — perhaps both involuntarily — to a Yeerk.

<My dear Inspector, perhaps you would like the honor of killing the Andalite scum before us. Wait. I have a better idea.>

Visser Three paused and swiveled his stalk eyes to look down contemptuously at his colleague. The animosity between the two was palpable, unmistakable.

<Because you seem to think it is so easy a task to eliminate these enemies of the Yeerk Empire,> the visser went on, <I challenge you to destroy these two pitiful samples. Right here. And right now.> He waved an arm broadly around, encompassing the pool. <I think it would be an inspiration to our brother Yeerks.>

<TokillthesepatheticEarthcreaturesisnochallengeforacreaturewiththespeedandskillofaGaratron,> the inspector answered.

<Rachel? Maybe now's not the time to ask, but — are the others with you?>

<You're right,> I said, every eagle muscle tense, my keen eyes watchful, boring into the inspector, hoping to anticipate a move. <It's a lousy time to ask. And the answer is, I don't know.>

Visser Three chuckled. A very disturbing sound. <My dear Inspector! Are you saying that you decline my challenge? I don't understand. You berate me for not having been successful in permanently subduing the Andalite bandits. And yet, when offered the opportunity to do so yourself, you refuse? I'm afraid I must take your refusal to mean an admission of . . .>

<Iacceptyourchallengethatisnochallenge,> the inspector spat.

<Cassie, get rea —>

ZZZIIISSSPPP!

A bluish blur that seemed to shoot through the air over the Yeerk pool.

The creature ran on water!

Whoooosh!

THUUWMPF!

<Aaahh!>

I was down!

Thwacked off Cassie's back by the Garatron's whiplash speed before I could even lift off!

I was on my back. Slightly stunned. I beat my wings madly against the steel pier, trying to right myself.

Whooooosh! Whooooosh!

The inspector zipped around and around Cassie, in an ever-tightening-then-widening circle. In and out, in and out. Amazingly fleet and sure-footed on the narrow pier.

Cassie, huge and suddenly cumbersome compared to her foe, smacked and batted the air with her massive paws. Hit nothing!

Reared up to her full height and swung the length of chain over her head —

FWUPFWUPFWUP!

— and let it fly!

SPUH-LOOSH!

Into the Yeerk pool!

<Rachel! I can't touch him!>

Whooooosh! Whooooosh!

Cassie batted again. Missed. Fell back to her four huge feet and swung her massive body around and —

<Aaahh!>

Her back right leg slipped off the edge of the pier! She scrambled back up, one paw wet and matted with sludgy gray liquid.

<I'll get him, Cassie! Keep him occupied!>

I was back on my feet. The air was not good for flying — for gaining altitude, getting high enough so that I could dive and attack.

But I had to try!

I was a bald eagle! A bird of prey that could spot darting fish beneath the surface of a river or lake at a thousand feet! A bird that could dive for that swimming fish — that moving target — and catch it, still alive and squirming, in my talons' strong grip.

I flapped — hard, harder, even harder.

Threw my body upward into the motion, willing myself to climb.

I rose off the slick surface of the steel pier where the inspector was still madly, untiringly circling Cassie, impossibly creating a whirlwind in the wet air, slowing only every few revolutions for less than half a split second to THWAP! her with his brutally fast tail.

A tail that was beginning to leave deep, bloody slashes along the polar bear's already lacerated flesh.

I rose into the damp mold-and-earth-smelling air.

Saw that all around us, ringing the pier and the pool like Romans cheering on the gladiators, were Controllers watching the inspector destroy my best friend.

Controllers led by Visser Three, evil emanating from his stolen Andalite body like the nauseating smell of sour milk.

It ticked me off.

A lot.

I had enough height, was maybe a few hundred feet above Cassie and the Garatron.

No Dracon beam sliced through the air to stop me. Obviously, the visser didn't want to interfere with this interesting event. This fight to the finish.

For a second I wondered who he was rooting for — his nemesis, the inspector, or the Andalite bandits.

Politics, I thought with disgust.

I targeted my prey. The moving target. The vague blue blur that was menacing my friend and making the lives of the Animorphs seriously un-comfortable.

I dove. Closer . . . closer.

Couldn't . . . there! Banked slightly . . . no . . .

Dive, dive!

Talons forward, big feathered legs stretched and eager!

Got him . . .

<Aaahhhh!>

<Rachel!>

WHUMPF!

I was down!

Smashing down onto the pier, twisting and wrenching my neck, bending back my left wing. Sliding! Coming to a bad stop inches from the end of the pier.

I'd missed, maybe only nicked the inspector's sleek Garatron head, maybe not.

I couldn't . . .

I was the hero. Warrior. King. And I couldn't defeat the enemy! Couldn't save my best friend.

Couldn't . . .

"Tseeeeer! Tseeeer!"

<Tobias!>

CHAPTER 21

"Tseeeer!"

Yes!

From the arched roof of the vast underground space that is the Yeerk bastion . . .

From what seemed to be the very center of the high dome, past the steel supporting beams, down, down past the high walls of dirt . . . came the cavalry.

A red-tailed hawk.

A northern harrier.

And in the talons of the hawk and the harrier — a cobra!

Fast, muscular, crushingly strong. A body that was nothing more and nothing less than a long and powerful whip.

118

A whip and a mouth that contained fangs and sacs of deadly poison.

Kinda the perfect morph for Marco, when you thought about it.

The Garatron came to a dead stop, somehow at the safe end of the pier. Out of reach of the injured bald eagle and dazed and bleeding polar bear.

<Aha!> Visser Three. <Why, here are a few more Andalite bandits coming now,> he boomed. <Are you feeling up to the challenge, Inspector?>

<YoumustcallmeCouncilor.>

<Oh, I will, you may be sure,> the visser said, his tone taunting, his voice thick with false emotion. <I will be honored to call you Councilor once you kill — eliminate — these pesky traitors to the Yeerk cause.> With a weak Andalite arm, the visser gestured grandly. Dramatically.

Mockingly.

<I promise on the lives of the Council of Thirteen,> he went on, <that the glory of the bandits' deaths will be yours. In fact, so grateful will I be when you succeed in this mission at which I have so miserably failed, I will voluntarily resign my post as Visser Three, leader of the Earth invasion, and throw my considerable support behind your ascension to the council.>

The inspector said nothing.

<And you will succeed in killing the bandits,

won't you, Inspector?> the visser said, his voice suddenly flat and cruel.

"Tseeeer!"

The inspector looked up. Shifted his hooves and seemed to tense when he saw the three Earth creatures so close, only yards above his head.

Once again, I struggled to my feet. Watched as Tobias and Ax released their dangerous burden within striking distance of the Garatron!

Who didn't zip away. Who looked down at the slowly wriggling creature. Dismissed it as unimportant. Looked upward.

To watch Tobias, flapping madly to regain some height. Then coming back around again, diving, talons outstretched, for the inspector.

The inspector moved, maybe only an inch or two, but so amazingly fast that Tobias missed. Circled, struggled for height again.

<Ax! Hurry!> I shouted.

Hork-Bajir! I hadn't heard the visser give an order but Hork-Bajir, ten or fifteen of them, were moving toward the Garatron from where they'd gathered around the cages of human-Controllers.

To his aid or . . . for a moment I wondered.

But the inspector's attention was riveted on Ax, who was demorphing to Andalite. And then, up, to the screeching, attacking bird . . .

<Ow! Don't these guys cut their toenails?>

Marco, being carelessly stepped on by a running Hork-Bajir. Then, more deliberately stomped . . .

<Get a clear shot, Marco!> I cried.

<Gee, I hadn't considered that option . . .>

ZZIIISSSPPP!

The Garatron was back in action. He dashed away from Marco's reach. Spun madly around Ax.

Fwapp! Fwapp! Fwapp!

Ax missed, every time.

<Keep him busy, Ax-man,> Marco ordered.

Slither, coil. Uncoil, scrunch. Forward, slow but sure.

The cobra advanced silently around the Hork-Bajir guards who had gathered in a loose ring around the battling inspector and Ax.

To make sure the inspector didn't walk away? To make sure he fought to the death? Whose death?

But their eyes weren't on the ground. Their eyes were on the spectacular, dizzying display of stunning speed before them. On the madly, futilely slashing young Andalite.

Slither, coil. Uncoil, stretch.

Closer and closer.

Close. Inches.

HSSSIIIPP!

Marco launched!

For a brief moment I saw more of the inspector than just a blue blur as Marco held one of his legs with his fangs. As he pumped killing poison into the Garatron's unsuspecting alien body.

Marco had struck the Garatron while he was moving at full speed. Like snatching a bullet out of the air.

<You're fast, Yeerk,> Marco said. <I'm faster.>

And then Marco released his victim, slithered, coiled, uncoiled, and stretched off behind the confused Hork-Bajir.

But still the Garatron ran!

<Oh no!> Cassie said. <What if the venom doesn't have an effect on the Garatron?>

<We've got to help Ax! Let's do it!>

But before Cassie and I could drag our battered bodies back up the pier and into the fray . . .

The Garatron! The inspector was slowing. Stumbling.

Still circling Ax, but his long tail drooping.

One slim front leg suddenly, awkwardly, entwined with the other.

<What is hap - pen - ing!> he cried, even his speech was slower, thicker as he came to a faltering, swaying stop.

<Are you experiencing a problem, my dear Inspector?> Visser Three boomed, his voice dripping phony concern.

<Cassie, now! Into the Yeerk pool and get to osprey or seagull,> I commanded. I didn't turn

around when I heard a smooth sliding dive behind me.

<Ax — you, too. Go bird, now! Everybody! I don't know what kind of macho game is going on with these two guys, but we are so out of here the second we get the chance!>

<You okay to fly, Rachel?> Tobias, still circling.

<Yeah. I'm okay. Just get Marco. And everybody, go out the way we came in.>

The inspector fell to his knees. And then rolled over onto his side. I rose into the air with difficulty and watched the Garatron's legs straighten, stiffen.

The ring of Hork-Bajir guards stood still. Silent and unmoving. Not going to the inspector's aid. Not making any attempt to stop Ax from finishing his morph. Not preventing Tobias from swooping down to grab Marco in his talons.

Too afraid to infuriate the visser by turning their attention to the polar bear in the Yeerk pool.

But the visser was watching and noticing everything.

<Inspector!> he cried. <Look! The Andalite bandits are getting away! You must go after them!>

<I . . . I cannot . . . move . . .> the inspector responded weakly, haltingly.

<Yes, and very, very soon you will not be able

to breathe,> Visser Three said matter-of-factly. <I will be sure to pass along your farewells to the Council. My dear Inspector.>

Slooop!

Cassie!

Rising from the sludgy gray Yeerk pool as seagull!

<Come on!> I cried, already giddy with the sense of victory, no matter how bizarre it was or in what strange way it had been gained.

We were going home. All of us.

CHAPTER 22

The sense of triumph didn't last. It never does. Real life is complicated. It gets in the way of nice, simple emotions.

I went to see the old man's grandson.

Maybe I would have gone to the funeral or something if they'd had it here. But the news said the man's family had flown his body back to his own hometown somewhere across the country for the funeral and burial.

"Interment," they said. Ugly word.

The news also said the old man had a history of serious heart trouble. That he was bound to die at any time. "Just any old time," his sister was quoted as saying.

Maybe going to the funeral would have been

easier. Probably. I could have sat at the back of the church or whatever and just paid my respects silently. Without having to come face-to-face with the man's grandkid.

Without having to say anything to him.

Like, "Gee, sorry your grandpa died. I'm kind of responsible, actually, so if you hate me or anything, that's okay. . . ."

I didn't say that.

I got the kid's phone number — easy enough — and spoke to his mom. The old man's daughter. I asked if I could come by and . . . I told her I'd been in the TV studio that day and seeing her father die had been really . . .

Somehow, she gave me permission to speak with her son. He was about Sarah's age.

He was okay with the death now.

At least, he seemed okay. I think he was kind of weirded out by having to talk to this strange blond girl while his mother watched and listened intently. Making sure I wasn't a whacko there to hurt her kid, I guess.

"I'm sorry," I finally said.

The kid shrugged. "Okay." And then he looked up at me. "Why?"

I tried to smile. I stood up. "I just am, I guess," I said. "I have to go now."

I raced out of that house so fast. And ran

straight into Jake, waiting at the end of the driveway.

"You're back."

Jake raised an eyebrow. "You noticed? Your powers of observation are really amazing, Rachel."

I grimaced and we turned toward our own neighborhood.

"You heard?" I asked. Very afraid of the answer.

Jake smiled. "Got home late last night. My dad turned on the late news. They're talking about 'escaped' wild animals busting up a TV studio, bunch of other places. A private jet doing a swan dive into a high rise. That all sounded like maybe some people I knew were involved."

"It was a big day."

"I figured I'd better call Cassie. She told me some of it. I talked to Marco, and he told me some more. They both said you'd probably want to tell me some stuff yourself."

"I don't want to tell you anything," I admitted. "But I guess I have to. I screwed up. Big time."

He walked in silence beside me for a while. "How many Animorphs were there when you started?"

"Six."

"And now?"

127

"Still six. Yeah, I didn't get anyone killed."

"Well, that's the first thing to do, you know: Don't get anyone killed. If it makes you feel better, the others think you did pretty well."

"Do they?" I thought for a moment. Kept my eyes forward. "We failed to get rid of the visser. Like Tobias said, we're back to the evil we know."

Jake laughed. "Yeah, well, Rachel, the visser's hard to get rid of. Doesn't mean we stop trying," he added.

"I know. Hey, maybe the Yeerks will reconsider the Garatrons' usefulness as hosts," I said hopefully. "At least for combat."

"I wouldn't be too sure we've seen the last of them."

"Aren't you Mr. Optimistic," I said, feeling a little deflated. Like the little bit of glory I'd taken away from the whole episode was not worth very much, after all.

"You did good, Rachel," Jake said simply. "You did what you had to do."

I stopped walking. I looked at Jake. "How do you do this? How do you make decisions that may get people killed? How do you live with that?"

"It's a war," he said. "We do what we have to do because we're forced to do it, right? Someday it will all be over. Someday the Andalites will come. Or the Yeerks will decide we're not worth it. Someday we'll win."

"Maybe. But how do you make decisions that get your friends hurt? That maybe someday will get us killed? How do you keep it from getting inside your head and just eating away at you?"

Then I saw something strange on his face. For just a fleeting moment it was the face of a terrified kid on the edge of tears. It shocked me. I knew what I was seeing. It was my face when I'd realized the old man had died. My face when I thought I'd lost Cassie forever.

But then the mask came down. And he was Jake again. "I don't think about it," he lied.

We walked on in silence for a few minutes.

"You okay?" Jake said finally.

I shook my head, as if to shrug off the question. "Yeah, you know. Um, Jake?"

We made a left at the end of the block and started to walk toward home, the setting sun at our backs.

"Yeah?"

"Don't ever, ever go away again."

Don't miss

#38 The Arrival

KEEERRRACCKKKK!

I leaped out of range before the tree limb could fall on me. The limb I had severed with one blow of my tail.

<Good shot!> Tobias circled downward, landing in the tree.

Tobias is interesting. A *nothlit*, but now an almost voluntary one. He has lost his human life, but not his human friends. He belongs. But at the same time, he does not belong.

Like me.

Perhaps that is why he is my true *shorm*. What humans would call a "best friend." Or "soul mate." That and the fact that my brother was Tobias's father.

I assumed the attack position again.

<Would you mind not doing that while I'm sitting here?> Tobias asked.

<They said they would find me. I may be called upon to fight at any moment. I must be ready. I must practice.>

Even though I am only an *aristh* — what humans would call a cadet — in the Andalite military, I had undergone rigorous training at the Academy. Tail fighting is a sport, an art, and a deadly combat skill.

I had a feeling that I was about to be tested. I did not want to disgrace myself.

<Okay. But you know, it also wouldn't hurt to take a look around town. See if there's any sign of Andalite troop presence. You know, maybe a couple dozen of your folks down at the mall. Besides, I found twenty bucks this morning. Which sounds like a visit to the food court to me.>

<Cinnabon?>

<Cinnabon for you. Me, I'm a taco kind of guy. When I'm not enjoying fresh mouse.>

Cinnamon buns!

I paused. I am extremely fond of cinnamon buns. I am so fond of them, it is hard for me to restrain my joy in eating them.

I have now had much practice eating cinnamon buns. But from time to time, I still have difficulty containing my enthusiasm for the taste sensations that come from these tasty treats.

This is one of the things I must explain to my people: the incredible joys of acquiring human morphs and using the mouth to ingest intensely flavored items.

I began to morph a northern harrier. The blue and tan fur of my body began to grow longer and shingle. Layer upon layer of feathers appeared upon my shrinking body.

<I take it that means yes — especially since I've already hidden our outer clothing on the mall roof,> Tobias said.

We flew over the main part of town. Together. But not close. If Tobias and I were seen flying in tandem, it might attract attention. Yeerk attention.

Once we had landed safely on the mall roof, Tobias began morphing to human.

The sharp angles of his scowling hawk head blurred and rounded out. Flesh appeared on his face first. It swirled and rippled like dough as it arranged itself into human eyes, a human nose, and a human brow.

His bird legs grew enormously long until what began to protrude was no longer bird leg, but bone. The bone formed a femur, a patella, and a tibia. Claws became toe bones.

Flesh poured down the bones like liquid and molded thighs, calves, and feet.

I concentrated. I would have to demorph to Andalite before morphing to human.

Though we have agreed that it is immoral to acquire the DNA of sentient creatures, we also have agreed upon exceptions now and then. I acquired a bit of DNA from Jake, Marco, Cassie, and Rachel. Thus, when I am human, I vaguely resemble all of them, but duplicate no one.

It is a moral compromise.

We have all learned to make them.

The question was how I could make such opportunities available to my fellow Andalites once they landed and defeated the Yeerks.

"Come on," Tobias said as soon as I had morphed from Andalite to human and was properly dressed in my artificial skins. "Let's hit the 'Bon and the Taco Bell."

I followed Tobias toward the small stairwell off the roof used by workmen. Through that door and down two flights of stairs was a door that led into the mall.

We heard the commotion the moment we entered the first floor. It was coming from the food court.

"Beanzuh! Beanzuh! Zuh!" I heard a girl shout.

"Somebody get security!" a woman yelled.

"What's going on?" someone else asked.

"Some girl went berserk in the food court," another person answered. "Eating everything in sight and yelling like a lunatic."

Tobias raised an eyebrow. "Which answers the question of whether the Andalites have landed."

We ran.

T 51628

DATE DUE

JUN 1 9 2003			
MAR 2 3 2004			

Demco, Inc. 38-293